Shoes on the Bridge

Meet the Family

Emerald A. Moore

DEDICATION

This book is dedicated to my son Miles, the youngest champion of the family.

"It is easier to build strong children than to repair broken men."
Frederick Douglas

To my beautiful niece, Lacey, who reminds me to thank God for everything from pretty lights to cupcakes!

ACKNOWLEDGMENTS

A special thank you to all of my family and friends for all of your enthusiasm and support throughout this journey.

Thank you Lioness for sharing your courage.

Above all, I am most thankful for the gifts of the Holy Spirit!

CHAPTER ONE

The hospital room was cold and very lonely. As Desiree reflected on her life with an abusive father and her abusive boyfriends, she wondered if this was all life had to offer her. Was there anything more she could expect for herself and her two year old son Gabriel?

After being abused by TJ, Desiree took their son and left him. Raising Gabriel without his father was hard, so when she met Romeo and he promised to take care of them, Desiree believed he was her knight in shining armor, only to discover Romeo was even more abusive than TJ.

Feeling alone and scared, she wanted so much to talk to Rena. Rena was the only true friend she had, and Rena was also the one friend she betrayed. With no one else to turn to, Desiree decided it was time to return Rena's call. Although they had not spoken in more than seven years; she still felt close to Rena; now all she could do was hope Rena really had forgiven her.

Desiree dialed Rena's number and tried to calm her

nerves as she waited for Rena to answer.

When Rena saw it was Desiree calling, she took a deep breath before answering. Rena could hear the nervousness in Desiree's voice.

"Desiree, I'm glad you finally returned my call," said Rena.

"I couldn't talk to you," answered Desiree. "You were such a good friend to me when everyone else in the neighborhood looked down on me. Actually you were more like my big sister than my friend, and Rena, I am so sorry," sobbed Desiree.

"I know," answered Rena. There was a long pause, then Rena asked, "Desiree, are you in trouble again?"

"Yes," replied Desiree in a soft tone. "It's Romeo. I can't get away from him. I don't know what else to do."

"Desiree, where is your son?"

"I left him with my mother; she doesn't know any of this, she has her own problems. My father has not changed, and she can't get away from him either."

"Desiree, what hospital are you in?"

"Mercy Hospital," she said.

"Okay" said Rena. "I'm on my way."

Rena dressed quickly and prayed as she made her way to her jeep. Seeing Desiree was sure to bring back old memories, but she knew God was dealing with her about forgiveness and at least she was taking the first step.

The drive to the hospital made Rena uneasy; she and Desiree had not seen each other in years and Rena often wondered how she would react if their paths ever crossed again, but she put those feelings aside and decided to be there for Desiree, just as she always had been in the past.

When Rena entered the room, Desiree was asleep. She stood and watched her friend for a few minutes.

Even with the scars on her face, Desiree was still just as pretty as she remembered. Desiree slowly opened her eyes.

"Rena?"

"My goodness, Desiree, what has that man done to you?"

Desiree cried again, and Rena rushed to the side of her bed and held her. "It's okay Desiree, don't cry."

"I don't know what to do Rena. I have no one to turn to. I can't keep doing this by myself."

"I know, Desiree, and you were on my heart heavily over the past few months. Now I want you to listen to me. You don't have to keep running from me. What happened between you and Mike happened years before I married him. From here on, we are going to work on our friendship and leave the past behind us. Will you let me pray for you," asked Rena.

Desiree managed to smile as she wiped the tears from her eyes.

"Rena, you haven't changed at all. Of course I will let you pray for me."

"Okay," said Rena. "Now let's get you some real help."

Rena held Desiree as she prayed with her, then the two friends spent the next three hours talking, laughing, and crying until the nurse told Rena that visiting hours were over. Desiree grabbed Rena's hand.

"I wish you didn't have to go."

"Don't worry, I'll be back tomorrow, I promise. Now, try and get some rest and think about what I told you. You can go to God just as you are; you don't need to get your life together first; that's one of the amazing things about God's love and His grace; it's available to everyone."

"Everyone?" asked Desiree.

"Yes" replied Rena. "Everyone; God is the master of

restoring broken people and broken relationships. Just talk to Him right from your bed. I promise you Desiree, He will hear you."

Rena reached over and gave Desiree a hug. At first Desiree decided not to ask Rena the one question she so desperately wanted to ask, but now that Rena was here with her, she felt safe. If Rena did not forgive her, she would not have come to the hospital to see her, so Desiree took a deep breath; she turned to Rena and said, "Rena, can I ask you something?"

"Of course," answered Rena.

"How are you able to forgive me for sleeping with Mike?"

Rena looked at Desiree for several minutes. When Rena did not reply right away, Desiree got scared, but Rena finally replied saying, "I told you God is a healer. I had to pray and ask God to help me, and it wasn't easy at first, but I do forgive you, Desiree. Now get some rest. I'll be back tomorrow."

With Rena gone, Desiree decided it was time to take her friend's advice.

"God if you can hear me, I want to ask you to help me, but how can I do that when I don't even know you? How can I believe a God that I can't see will accept me and protect me when my own father never did? The only person who cares about me is the one friend I hurt the most, but if Rena can forgive me after what I have done, then there must be some truth to what she says about you."

Desiree closed her eyes. Fighting through the tears she continued to pray, "God, if it's true that you will accept me just as I am, and you don't care how badly I messed up; and if it's true that you can heal my pain, and love and protect me, then please come into my life. I just can't keep doing this by myself anymore!"

Desiree did not know what to expect after she prayed but she did feel a sense of peace, and this time when she closed her eyes, she was not afraid. This time she closed her eyes and she believed God was watching over her.

CHAPTER TWO

Rena woke to find her husband up and ready for work; she still could not understand Mike's crazy hours. He was either going in early and working late or going in late and working even later; either way the result was the same, Mike was never home. This was the second issue that fueled her anger; his one-night fling with Desiree was the first. Their marriage was anything but ideal.

As his shower came to an end, Rena pulled the blanket up to her chin and held it tightly. Today was her birthday, and she wanted Mike to stay home; for once she wanted to be on his list of priorities but as usual, Mike had other plans.

"Good morning, birthday girl," Mike cheered while throwing himself on their bed. Mike playfully pulled the covers back and tried to kiss his wife. Rena smiled and gave him a gentle kiss. "Here, this is for you, go ahead and open it." Rena untied the ribbon from the small box. At least he was sticking around long enough to acknowledge my birthday, she thought to herself. As she opened the box she gasped at the beautiful gold necklace with a small cross hanging from it. "Oh, Mike, it's beautiful!"

"I'm glad you like it," he said, hopping off of the bed. Now don't forget to arrive at Carl's house by four o'clock.

The guests should arrive by five o'clock, and I'll get there as soon as I can."

Mike secured his badge to his jacket, then placed his gun in the holster and walked over to Rena. "You are beautiful; you know that, don't you?" Rena stood up and hugged him. "Please don't be late tonight Mike. This is my party, and I want my husband there with me, on time!" Mike gave her a quick kiss on the cheek and then headed out the door.

Rena sat on the bed and carefully placed her gift back in the box. Today she turned thirty-four, but she was not happy. Being unable to conceive and married to a man who found every reason to be anywhere but home was not her dream come true.

The phone interrupted Rena's thoughts; she leaned over and saw it was Desiree calling, and she decided not to answer. It didn't seem fair; she had spent the past several days helping Desiree take care of her son while she recovered from Romeo's abuse, but her own arms remained empty. Rena wiped a tear from her face. "No," she said out loud. "I'm not going to let this get to me. Today is my birthday, and I plan to enjoy it." Rena decided to call her mother and tell her about her gift and the party Mike had planned for her, but it didn't take her mother long to rain on her parade.

"That's so sweet, honey. I'm glad you're happy with your birthday present, but honestly, I don't understand why Mike would give you a birthday party in someone else's house. Is there something you're not telling me? You and Mike still have your own home, don't you?"

"Mom, why on earth would you ask me a question like that? Of course we still have our home."

"Well, why didn't your husband just invite your friends there?"

"I told you Mom, Carl's backyard is big enough to

hold all the guests Mike invited, and this is a good way for Carl to meet some new people. He's been in Atlanta almost five years now and hardly knows anyone."

Rena's mother contemplated her thoughts. "So is there anyone in particular you and Mike are hoping to set Carl up with? That is one good looking man!"

Rena laughed as she held up a dress she considered wearing. "Not really. We managed to invite several single women, but I honestly can't see Carl with any of them."

"Well, I hope Jenna is not on the guest list," she replied. "That girl is just as mean as her mother was."

"Jenna's not so bad mom; and you're acting like Jenna's a stranger. Remember we all lived and grew up in the same neighborhood. Besides, Mike planned a very nice party and I want all of my friends there. I even invited Jay."

"Poor Jay, growing up with a mean mother and sister, no wonder she drinks so much. Who else did Mike invite?"

"No one else you know except for Cookie. You remember her from college?"

"Yes," replied her mother. "I never cared much for her either."

Rena rolled her eyes; her mother was so draining. "Mom, I have to go. I'll call you tomorrow and let you know how everything turned out."

"Okay honey, enjoy yourself and don't be too hard on your husband, you know that's the quickest way to send him into the arms of another woman."

Rena sighed; "Goodbye, mother."

With so much going on she started to wonder if inviting Jenna and Jay was a mistake. Her mother was right, Jenna was toxic and Jay always managed to cause a scene after a drink or two, but there was nothing she could do about it now. She spent the next few hours getting ready, and then headed out to pick up Jenna. As she drove Rena could only hope Jenna would be in a good mood. Mike did not even want Jenna at the party but she insisted on inviting her; now she hoped she would not regret it.

Fortunately, when she arrived, Jenna was standing outside and flashed a smile when she saw her. Rena felt a sense of relief. If Jenna was smiling that meant she was in a good mood, at least for the moment.

The drive to Druid Hills took Jenna by surprise; although she was familiar with this part of Atlanta, she could not believe Rena and Mike actually knew anyone who lived there.

As Rena's truck pulled into Carl's driveway, Jenna marveled at the beautifully landscaped lawn.

"I hope we're not late," said Rena. "I can't imagine why all these cars are already here."

"Don't worry about it, Rena. You're the birthday girl; they can't start without you."

"That's right," said Rena. "Come on, let's go inside, and don't forget the fruit salad."

As they walked up the long driveway, Jenna quickly became suspicious. "What did you say this man did for a living?" she asked.

"He's a college professor," replied Rena.

"I didn't know college professors made this kind of money; in fact, I know they don't make this kind of money."

Rena was becoming annoyed with her already. "Carl teaches economics," she replied. "But he also wrote several books, including two textbooks the university uses."

Jenna shrugged her shoulders before replying, "Most people have ghost writers, so he probably did not write the books himself."

"Whatever," replied Rena. "Just be nice and watch what you say to him. Carl is Mike's best friend, but he has a very low tolerance for nonsense. Keep your negative comments to yourself, and by all means keep an eye on Jay; the last thing I need is for her to act up in here."

"Oh please, Rena, you are always worried about what people think. I could care less about Mike's friend, and if you were so worried about Jay acting up, you should not have invited her, besides; Desiree is the one you should be worried about. At least Jay didn't sleep with your husband. I still can't believe you could forgive Desiree for that. I can't stand that girl; I remember how she looked at Maurice."

Rena gave Jenna a doubtful stare. "You mean how Maurice looked at her."

"Whatever," replied Jenna, while struggling to hold the large bowl of fruit salad. "I still don't trust her."

Rena was becoming more annoyed with Jenna. Her mother kept telling her it was time for her to dump Jenna and Jay; she said some childhood friends are better left as memories and she was right.

As they approached the gate to Carl's backyard, Rena's cell phone rang and Jenna became irritated; the bowl of fruit salad was heavy, and she needed to put it down. A young woman on her way into the party noticed Jenna struggling to hold the heavy bowl and she motioned for Jenna to follow her inside. Jenna followed the woman inside and immediately began looking around for her sister Jay. As she strolled through the crowd, she felt a set of eyes staring at her. Glancing over her shoulder, she noticed a tall, dark-skinned man dressed in khaki shorts and a yellow T-shirt; He was standing over the grill and appeared to have one eye on the food and the other on her. Jenna was certain that was Carl; everything she heard about Carl fit the description of the man who was now boldly staring at her. Excitement and curiosity replaced her irritated mood and she quickly dismissed any thoughts of leaving Rena's party early; she now had a reason to stay.

Thirty minutes later, Rena finally made her entrance into the party, but she was alone. Jenna stared at her friend and wondered why she thought tonight would be any different. It was the same old story. Mike was always working. She watched quietly as her friend glided through the arms of her guests while making excuses for Mike's absence. When she could no longer stand the sight of Rena pretending to be the happy hostess, she decided to try and mingle with Rena's guests. Jenna introduced herself to a group of women from Rena's church and was surprised at how easily they welcomed her. After several minutes she found herself laughing so hard she could hardly contain herself. This must be why her grandmother said laughter was such good medicine. Eventually, the talk moved from humorous conversation to church events, and Jenna quickly became bored; she excused herself and headed for the buffet table. There was so much food displayed she wasn't sure where to begin, but the strong aroma coming from the brick barbeque pit caught her attention, and she began sampling the skewed shrimp covered in mango sauce before moving on to an amazing grilled pasta dish covered in roasted peppers. With her stomach full she decided to walk around; with any luck she would run into Carl and introduce herself.

After a few minutes she spotted him carrying a tray of lobster tails to the table, but before she could make her way to him, she noticed Jay dancing alone on the patio. Jay held the end of her skirt in one hand and a martini in the other. If her dance moves didn't confirm the fact that she had too much to drink, the words to the song she butchered certainly did. Jay was loud and off tune, but no one else seemed to care so Jenna decided to leave her alone. Suddenly the music shifted into a salsa tune and Jay threw her martini onto the floor and began clapping and yelling while trying to dance to the salsa tune. Carl quickly put down the tray of lobster tails and joined Jay in a salsa move that had everyone clapping and cheering them on. Jenna laughed as she watched Carl take the lead with Jay. It was obvious he was no stranger to salsa music, which was a good thing since Jay had no idea what she was doing. As the crowd circled around Carl and Jay, Jenna turned her attention to a heavyset woman dressed in white spandex pants, a gold-and-black tank top, and a pair of gold-and-black Gladiator sandals that boosted a six-inch heel. It did not take Jenna long to realize that the woman with her flashy attire and bold personality, was Rena's friend Cookie. Cookie boldly made her way through the crowd and took Jay by the hand before announcing to everyone that she was taking over the dance. Cookie led Jay away from Carl and delivered her into the crowd while the guests laughed. Jenna could not believe her sister allowed herself to be humiliated like that. Instead of Jay standing her ground with Cookie, she simply walked through the crowd asking if anyone knew where her drink was. Jenna burned with anger as she watched Cookie shake her shoulders while swinging her body from side to side. Each step she took toward Carl drew more excitement and cheers from the crowd. Jenna stood by and watched as the so-called conservative college professor grabbed Cookie by her waist and spun her around, causing her eighteen-inch ponytail to nearly clip the bystanders.

When their dance finally ended, Carl reached for a bottle of water while Cookie wiped the sweat from his temples. Jenna waited for Cookie to turn around, then she attempted to intimidate her with a scornful look, but Cookie was not moved. Instead of backing away from Carl, she took the bottle of water out of Carl's hand and drank it. Cookie and Jenna engaged each other in a lengthy stare until Jenna gave in and stormed off.

Rena's party was now in full swing and Mike still had not shown up. Rena continued on with her warm and gracious routine, but inside she was boiling with anger. This night belonged to her, and once again her husband failed to come through for her. This was not the celebration she had hoped for.

Rena's disappointing evening went from bad to worse when she saw Jay emptying a bottle of alcohol into the barbeque pit. As the pit began to fill with smoke, Jay's fiancé, Luther quickly put out the small fire, then he tried to persuade Jay to go inside and sober up, but Jay would not go quietly. Rena watched nervously as Luther and Jenna struggled to get Jay inside the house. Fortunately, the basement had a separate entrance, and she helped them push Jay inside.

"Come on, Jay" said Rena. "I know what your problem is; you need to sober up a bit."

Jay stood up and replied, "And you know what your problem is, Rena? You're an idiot!"

Jay managed to take another sip of her drink before being whisked into one of the bedrooms by Jenna and Rena.

"Shut your mouth, right now Jay!" ordered Jenna as she removed Jay's drink from her hand.

"Leave me alone, Jenna. I'm telling the truth, and you know it. Desiree slept with Rena's husband, and she wants everyone to think things are okay, but she's still mad. That's why your husband's not here Rena; he can't stand to be around you."

"First of all, Jay, what happens between Mike and me is none of your business, and for your information, that fling with Desiree happened way before we were married."

Jay managed to wiggle out of Jenna's grip. "It doesn't matter how long ago he slept with her; a scorned woman owns no clock!" Jay tried to maintain her balance as she stood up and asked, "Where is my drink, and where did Luther go?" "That's a good question," answered Rena. "I'm going to find your fiancé and have him take you home." Rena stormed out of the basement and into the night air. The last thing she needed was to hear Jay bringing up a part of Mike's past that she struggled to deal with; she was so sorry she ever invited Jay.

After ten minutes, Jenna grew tired of waiting for Luther to come back, she needed to get back to the party and stop Cookie from getting her hands on Carl. Jenna pulled Jay's drink off the table and handed it back to her. Luther would have to worry about getting Jay home; right now she had more important things to worry about, so she left her sister alone and headed back out to the party.

Jenna stood outside the basement door for several minutes; she could not believe the amount of people that turned out for Rena's party. After planning the best way to get through the crowd, Jenna began walking around, and after several trips around the yard, she found Carl on the deck refilling the punch bowl. Carl lifted his head just in time to see the woman who caught his attention earlier approaching him.

"Carl?" she asked politely, extending her hand to him.

"No, I'm sorry; you must have the wrong person."

Jenna quickly withdrew her hand, but Carl pulled it

back. "I'm just teasing," he said. "I'm Carl, and you are?" Jenna was not impressed with his sense of humor; she did not like being the butt of anyone's joke, and she gave Carl a cold stare. "Look, I just wanted to introduce myself and thank you for having me in your home. Rena and I have been friends for years, and it would have been very rude of me to not acknowledge you as the host of her party."

"Look, I'm sorry if I offended you," replied Carl. "Are you always so serious?"

Jenna was through with him; the last thing she needed was a sarcastic, egotistical jerk putting the moves on her. She began to walk away when she heard Carl ask, "So where has Rena been hiding you?" Jenna turned around, trying not to let him see her smile, but Carl noticed and said, "Oh, wait a minute, what's this? Could it be a smile coming from one so serious?" "I'm sorry," said Jenna. "I guess we got off to a bad start. Can we try this again?"

Carl could not believe how taken he was with her. The long yellow dress she wore complemented her dark skin and her brown eyes. Jenna's hair was cut short, and she smelled so good Carl could hardly stand it. He continued to discretely look her over as he engaged her in conversation. Several minutes later Carl selected a song on the Bose system and led her onto the cobblestone patio for a dance.

"I'm not much of a dancer," pleaded Jenna.

"I don't care," he answered while starting to dance without her. Jenna started to protest again, but Carl was quick to inform her that it was very bad manners to insult the host twice in one night, so she agreed. When Carl wrapped his arms around her, Jenna thought she would melt in his arms. It had been four years since Maurice broke her heart by announcing his wedding date on the night he broke up with her. Clearly, their ten-year relationship meant more to her than it did to him.

Carl bent down and whispered in her ear, "Are you okay?"

"I'm fine," she replied. "I'm just worried about my sister."

"Well, then I must be doing something wrong," he said.

"What do you mean?" she asked.

"Here I am trying to get all of your attention while your mind is on your sister; that means I must be doing something wrong."

Jenna smiled and rested her head on his shoulder. "You're doing just fine."

The sun gave way to the evening dusk, and Mike finally arrived at his wife's celebration. As the door to his jeep slammed shut, Rena raced to her husband and threw her arms around him.

"Where have you been?" she whispered in his ear. Mike took her by the hand and escorted her into the backyard, never bothering to answer her question. As they made their way into the party, Mike looked around, the turnout was remarkable but he was not surprised, everyone loved Rena, she was warm, kind and loving and people were drawn to her.

With Mike finally in attendance, the Johnson sisters were ready to bring out Rena's birthday cake. Carl stood on his deck drinking his beer and taking advantage of finally having some time to himself. He did not realize how much planning went into hosting this party, but he was glad to do it. Although this was Rena's party, Carl felt he was the one who needed this celebration more. His heart still ached for his late wife, but tonight he felt a new chapter of his life opening up. Most of the guests were here for Rena, but there were several of his students, co-workers, and church friends who attended the party at his request. With new friends, a new job, and a new home, Carl realized his happiness was being restored, and maybe, just maybe he could fall in love again.

Carl finished his beer then stepped down from the deck and joined the group as they sang a lively birthday melody to Rena.

It was close to midnight, and Mike and Rena were preparing to leave when Jenna approached them. "I'm surprised you two are leaving already; shouldn't you stay and help Carl clean up?"

"We tried to," replied Rena. "The Johnson sisters took care of most of the cleaning up, and then Cookie jumped in and insisted on handling the rest. Cookie would love nothing more than to get her hands on Carl, and tonight she's pulling out all the stops; first she'll help clean his house, and then she'll move in."

Rena laughed as she walked away, totally oblivious to Jenna's hurt reaction. Didn't Rena see what happened between her and Carl? How could she make such a comment? The thought of Cookie setting herself up in Carl's house threw Jenna into a state of panic. She stormed past the handful of guests making plates to take home and marched up the stairs leading into the house. Jenna pulled back the sliding door, and her heart immediately sank. Standing over the sink washing dishes was Cookie, dressed in a pair of tight cut-off shorts and a very low-cut blouse that intentionally exposed her breasts. Cookie looked over at Jenna, and then ran her eyes up and down Jenna's tall frame before turning back to the dishes. Jenna was about to speak when Cookie turned off the water, placed one hand on her hip, and turned toward her. "Do you need something, honey? All the guests have left, and I hate to be rude, but Carl and I are ready to call it a night. I'm sure you can see your way out?" Cookie smiled at Jenna as she started wiping down the counter. Jenna studied Cookie briefly; she wasn't sure she believed her; after all, why would Carl have gone to all the trouble of asking her out if he was already involved with Cookie? Jenna was angry and speechless, but she refused to give Cookie the satisfaction of knowing she had upset her; she quickly turned and headed back out through the sliding door and stood on the deck for several minutes. It was too hard to ignore Cookie's comments; she needed to find Carl and get to the bottom of what was happening. As she looked out over the deck, all she could see was Mike folding up tables and Rena still wrapping up food for her guests to take home. There was no sign of Carl. As soon as the last table was folded and the remaining chairs were bought inside, Mike rushed Rena along and signaled for Jenna to come down from the deck; clearly he was ready to leave. Jenna responded back with a glare. How dare he show up several hours late to his wife's party and then rush to leave. Jenna ignored Mike's gesture. There was no way she was leaving without settling the score with Cookie first, so she turned and went back into the house. This time Cookie was fixing her ponytail, she rolled her eyes as Jenna approached her.

"Tell Carl I will see him tomorrow and that I am looking forward to our brunch date," boasted Jenna.

Cookie never took her eyes off her hand held mirror when she replied, "Oh, are you coming too?" Jenna was not prepared for Cookie's quick comeback, and once again she stormed out of the house defeated. Jenna marched down the stairs, snatched her punch bowl off the table, and yelled to Rena that she was ready to go.

Cookie breathed a sigh of relief when she saw Jenna get into Mike's jeep, and the jeep sped off. The only other car remaining in the driveway was Rena's truck, and that was parked there for the night. Cookie began to wonder what Carl would actually do if he found her still in his home. She had only come in to use the bathroom when she noticed Jenna right behind her and decided to have a little fun with her. Pleased with her little skit, Cookie chuckled at how easy it was to unnerve her. Suddenly, she heard the basement door slam shut, and she realized Carl was on his way back upstairs. Carl was not the type of man to fall for her games, and she knew things would not end well if he found her in his kitchen, so she grabbed her purse and slipped out.

⚜

Mike barely got the jeep into Jenna's driveway before she opened the door and got out, slamming the door behind her. Mike looked at his wife. "What's wrong with her?"

"Could be anything," replied Rena.

"Jenna, are you okay?" he asked while running to catch up to her.

"No," she snapped. "What's up with your friend? Does he make it a habit of asking one woman out while planning to sleep with another?"

Mike was shocked; he had no idea Carl was that serious about anyone. He ran up and blocked Jenna's path. "Look, Jenna, I don't know what Carl said or did, but I'm sure he didn't mean to upset you."

"Oh really? Then he's just into playing games with people? Well if it was his intention to play me for a fool, you can tell him, I am not the one. And what about your wife? Did she have to throw Carl's fling in my face?"

"Now wait a minute, Jenna, I'm sure Rena didn't mean to throw anything in your face. You know how Rena is; she would never do anything to hurt you."

"Of course you would protect her; she's your precious, perfect wife who lets you walk all over her! If you pulled half the crap with any other woman that you pull with Rena, you would be a single man by now! I don't know why Rena puts up with you, but if your friend thinks he's going to make a fool out of me, just like you do with Rena, then he better think again. Rena may be a submissive wife, but no man is going to make a fool out of me."

Mike had heard enough; he turned and walked back toward his jeep, but Jenna ran behind him, hurling insults and screaming so loudly that Mike became embarrassed. What he wouldn't give to slap a muzzle on Jenna. As she continued her verbal assault on him, Mike turned toward her, and with one finger in her face he shouted, "That right there is why Carl decided to spend the night with someone else. You are too angry to be a source of comfort to anyone!" Mike hurried back to his jeep and drove off, leaving Jenna standing in her driveway.

Mike was still agitated as he drove and Rena knew this was not the time to question him about getting to the party so late. She turned on the radio, hoping it would help to lighten the mood, but as soon as she found a song to listen to, Mike reached over and turned the radio off. Rena turned to him, but she did not say a word. She could not believe Mike would allow Jenna to get him so upset and she wondered if something more was upsetting him, but she did not bother to ask. Mike was not the type of man to talk about his feelings and she learned a long time ago, it was better to just wait and let Mike talk whenever he was ready, so they rode home in complete silence.

When Mike pulled into the garage Rena watched quietly as he stormed out of the jeep and into the house. He headed upstairs to take his shower without saying a word. Her birthday celebration was amazing and now thanks to Jenna, her evening with her husband was ruined; but Jenna was not her biggest concern. Rena had something more important on her mind, like where her husband had been between the time he left work and the time he showed up to her party. Those unexplained three hours were hard to ignore.

The night was long and hot, and now it started to rain. Rena's party was a huge success and Carl could not remember the last time he had so much fun. Only now, the party was over and he was alone again. Carl lay in his bed and began thinking about Lisa. It had been five years since Lisa's boating accident, and the rain reminded him of his late wife. Whenever it rained at night, Lisa would open the bedroom windows, light some candles, and cuddle up next to him, and they would spend hours talking. Things were so different now; Lisa was gone, and Carl spent the last five years trying to put his life back together again. He missed her terribly, but leaving Chicago gave him a chance to start over. He was so grateful for the family and friends God had placed in his life; without them he would not have survived the pain. The day of Lisa's funeral, the weather was cold and windy; but Carl was so hurt, he felt numb. He remembered thanking everyone for coming; and asking his father to please take his mother home after the service. Carl just wanted to be alone, but Mike refused to leave his side. Carl remembered standing by

Lisa's grave for two hours, battling the cold Chicago wind; and Mike stood there right beside him; never saying a word, just shivering and waiting patiently with him.

Tonight, Carl realized just how much his heart had healed. He was enjoying his life again. He kept in touch with his friends from Chicago and made new ones in Atlanta. Everything from his career to his new church family and friends told him, moving to Atlanta, was the right thing to do. The biggest surprise came when he realized with so many single women in his home, Jenna was the only one who strolled in and left with a piece of his heart. Carl thought it would be years before he would ever be able to look at a woman the way he looked at Jenna. While he had to admit, he hardly knew her, he was quick to notice she was very well educated and attractive. But he also noticed Jenna had her heart guarded; she appeared to be a strong woman, but she was clearly hurt; getting Jenna to trust him was going to be a challenge, but he didn't mind. Carl was willing to put in the time and work to prove himself, if that was what she needed.

Carl smiled as he began to think about their date tomorrow, then he reached over and turned off the lamp. He could hardly wait to see Jenna again.

CHAPTER THREE

Jenna woke up angry, she spent the whole night thinking about Cookie spending the night with Carl, but she was not ready to admit defeat. If Carl was attracted to women like Cookie, then that was the type of woman she would become. Jenna purchased a new dress for their date. Unlike the modest yellow dress she wore the day before, today's outfit would make a new statement; she showered using her most expensive body crème, then struggled into a white double-knit spandex dress with a bare back and thigh-high slits on the side. The dress tied around the neck and exposed more of her breasts than anyone needed to see. Jenna smoothed her hair, sprayed on perfume, and stepped back to view herself in the full-length mirror. Satisfied with what she saw, she grabbed a sweater she had no intention of wearing and headed out the door.

Driving down the highway, she felt her heart racing with excitement and a bit of nervousness. This was not her usual attire, and she was not at all comfortable in the dress; in fact, her seven-hundred-dollar shoes were the only part of her outfit she recognized, but if this was what Carl wanted, she was happy to oblige him.

As she made her way into the restaurant, she was surprised at how crowded it was. Looking around, she was impressed with the ambiance of the restaurant.

Exotic fish made their home in the manmade lake, and the pier was home to some of the most luxurious boats she had ever seen. Judging from the décor, she could tell the restaurant catered to a very conservative clientele. As Jenna patiently waited for the host, she began to feel very uneasy. Her dress did not fit the conservative attire most of the women wore, but there was nothing she could do about it now. Looking around she noticed a tall and fairly slim man dressed in a mustard-yellow polo shirt, long brown plaid shorts, and leather sandals and realized it was Carl; his clothes were a bit too relaxed for her taste, but he did say the dress was casual. Carl was standing at a table talking to a tall, distinguished-looking man whose skin bore the marks of red sunburn. The man was strong in stature, and his gray and white hair reflected the wisdom his demeanor possessed. Jenna quickly determined his level of importance, which was confirmed by the proud way he wore his military attire. Seated at his table was his wife, whose six-carat diamond-studded wedding band was hard to ignore. As she followed the host to Carl's table, she could not ignore the disapproving look she received from the woman with the ring. Almost as if he read the look on the woman's face, Carl turned to see what was wrong, and there was Jenna, walking toward him in a tight, breast-bearing dress. Jenna reached up to hug Carl, but he stepped back and gave her a questionable look. "Well, are you just going to stand there?" she asked. "You look like you just saw a ghost or something."

The older gentleman continued standing as he waited for Carl to introduce Jenna. Carl cleared his throat, made the introductions, then quickly excused himself and escorted Jenna to their table. As soon as they sat down, Carl noticed a group of old men boldly glaring over at Jenna as if he were not even there. Carl wanted nothing more than to walk over and wipe the lustful grins right off their faces, but instead he waited for the waiter to return, and he asked to be moved to a table in the rear. The waiter reluctantly agreed and escorted them to an area next to the smokers' lounge.

The first thing Jenna noticed about this area was how cold and isolated it was. It looked more like a cigar lounge than anything else, and it lacked the ambiance that made the rest of the restaurant so beautiful. The waiter stopped in front of a small wooden table with a white linen cloth and two wooden chairs that faced the outside garden. There were no fish in the small pond that sat in the center of the garden. The rest of the garden was gated and Jenna wondered what they were trying to preserve, since the garden itself seemed so bare. Jenna gave the waiter a disapproving look when she realized this was where he was seating them. The waiter turned to Carl, "I'm sorry, Sir, but this really is the best table in this section, and I must inform you there is no smoking in this area, in spite of the location."

"Thank you," said Carl as he walked over and pulled Jenna's chair out for her.

By now, Jenna was starting to feel uncomfortable; Carl treated her like an unwelcomed stranger. The disapproving look she gave the waiter could not compare to the icy stare Carl bestowed on her. She tried to pretend it did not bother her, but Jenna would give anything to be back in her long yellow dress right now. She wondered where the ladies room was, but quickly decided against getting up to find it, there was no need to give Carl a second preview of her outfit, when it was obvious he did not like her dress. Carl shook a napkin loose then leaned toward her, "You look very different, Jenna."

"What is that supposed to mean?" she asked.

"Just what I said, you look very different. I did tell you the dress here was casual, didn't I?"

Now Jenna was clearly insulted. "You know, Carl, it's very cold back here. The table we had was fine. I don't know why you asked to be moved."

Carl picked up his menu before replying, "Why don't you put your sweater on if you're cold?"

Jenna could not believe Carl's demeanor; yesterday he could not get enough of her, and today he was watching her as if she had stolen something. "Did you get much sleep last night?" she asked.

At first Carl thought she was being considerate, but he quickly noted the sarcasm in her voice. "Actually, I didn't get much sleep at all. I had a hard time unwinding."

Jenna frowned at him. "You mean to tell me Cookie's treats didn't do the trick?"

Carl slowly sipped his coffee. "What treats are you referring to, Jenna?"

"Do I really have to spell it out for you, Carl? Are you really going to make me say it?"

"Look, Jenna, I'm not into playing games, and you obviously have something on your mind, so why don't you just come out with it."

Jenna sat back in her chair, and breathed a sigh of relief. Finally she was able to lure Carl into an argument; her plan was to catch him in a lie, if he tried to deny spending the night with Cookie, make him beg for her forgiveness and then she would lay out a list of ground rules he needed to follow, if he wanted to see her again.

As the waiter walked by holding a tray of hot soup, Jenna rudely reached out and grabbed his arm, then asked him if he would take a few minutes from running around to come and take their order. Carl gave her a disapproving look for speaking so harshly to the waiter, but Jenna did not seem to care. They placed their order then sat in silence as Carl ignored the several attempts Jenna made to engage him into an argument.

When the food arrived, Carl began eating his steak right away while Jenna picked over her crab cakes and eggs before deciding not to eat any of it.

"Is something wrong with your food?" Carl asked.
"No, it's not the food, it's the company. I did not get up early and agree to have brunch with you, so that you could ignore me" she replied.

"Well, you're free to leave anytime you like," responded Carl.

As time went on, Jenna became more irritated by Carl's silence, and when he refused the pastry and coffee the waiter tried to serve, Jenna knew her plan had fallen apart. Carl looked very different to her too. He was not the handsome, funny, college professor she so easily fell for the night before. Carl was icy cold, very abrupt and very judgmental. Rena warned her about him, saying Carl had a low tolerance for nonsense, but this was not nonsense, Carl was simply being rude to her.
Jenna was still drinking her tea when Carl asked for the check; her heart sank as she realized Carl was ready to end the date. "I guess we should get going," he said. "I think we both missed out on some much needed sleep."

Jenna watched him shove a pile of cash into the black case. "So we're not having dessert?" she asked.
"Oh, I forgot you had Cookie's dessert last night, didn't you?" Carl began to anxiously search for the waiter. He could not imagine why Jenna thought he had spent the night with Cookie, and he wasn't sure he even cared. At this point, all he wanted to do was to get away from Jenna. Yesterday she seemed so poised and polished; she was a glamour girl with a brain. Today, he wasn't sure who Jenna was. How could he have misjudged this

woman? "Carl, I asked you a question. Are you going to answer me or do you just plan to sit there? Did you really think you were going to play me that easily? Well, let me tell you something."

"I don't have time for this nonsense, Jenna. There's enough money in that case to cover the check and tip." Carl threw his napkin on the table, picked up his jacket, and walked out of the restaurant. Jenna sat there for a few minutes, too embarrassed to move. When she thought no one was watching, she picked up her purse and her sweater, and with her head held down, she exited the restaurant.

CHAPTER FOUR

The next morning Carl woke and sat out in his front yard to have his coffee. His date with Jenna turned out to be a disaster, and he wasn't really sure why. Jenna's appearance threw him for a loop, but it was her attitude that made him lose interest in her. He leaned back in his lounge chair and began to read his newspaper, when his eyes caught glimpse of a silver four-door sedan approaching his driveway. Believing someone was lost and in need of directions, he stood up and walked toward the car. It only took him a minute to realize the car in his driveway belonged to Jenna. She began pressing on the horn, and she ordered him to come over and talk to her. Carl folded his newspaper under his arm and slowly approached the car. "What do you want, Jenna?"

"Talk to me," she demanded. "You had no right to leave me in the restaurant like that!"

Jenna got out of her car and slammed the door. Carl remained cautiously calm. In spite of his military training and his two degrees, he still felt he was no match for this lunatic standing in front of him. "I just want to talk about yesterday," she begged. "I know all about your night with Cookie, and I can let it go as long as it doesn't happen again."

"Listen to me, Jenna, I don't know where you got

your information, and it really doesn't matter. Now I am going to say this one time; I am not interested in taking this any further. I don't want to see or hear from you again, now get back in your car and get off of my property."

Jenna wanted to cry, but she refused to let Carl see how hurt she was. Fighting back the tears, she turned and hurried into her car and drove off. As soon as she was away from him, she allowed the tears to flow steadily down her face. Everything she did to impress Carl had gone wrong, and there was no way to fix it. How could he be so cruel to her? She pulled her car over and sat for a few minutes, trying to compose herself. Jenna remembered her mother's warning; she told her and Jay that all men were selfish and just wanted a woman they could use. Her mother did very little to raise them and the only time she offered any advice was to criticize their father or men in general. Jenna always knew her mother was bitter, but now she was convinced, her mother was probably right; men were just no good. Maurice proved it once, and Carl just confirmed it. Jenna dried her eyes and started the car.

At that very moment she decided to channel her anger elsewhere. Her boss Agatha bought in a new aspiring writer named Courtney. Jenna did not know much about her except that she was pretty much alone. Having grown up in foster care, Courtney came to Atlanta in search of her father. The young lady was sharp and talented; the fact that she was also very pretty made Jenna dislike her even more. Jenna was the best Fashion Editor in the company and while she did not have much success in relationships, Jenna was very successful in securing interviews and covering high profile fashion venues; her salary along with the respect she gained from the industry was all she had to show for her success; now having lost Carl to Cookie, she was not about to lose her spotlight at work to Courtney, so she decided to go into the office and see what assignments Courtney was working on. If Courtney even looked at one of her assignments, Jenna would make her sorry she ever came to work there. With so much competition in this industry, Jenna knew she could not afford to let her guard down.

As soon as she pulled into her parking spot, she headed for the coffee shop in the lobby, ordered a bagel and a cup of coffee and headed upstairs. As she made her way to the sixth floor, she was relieved to find the office locked. Agatha only allowed her top editors to have keys to the office and Jenna was proud to be part of that privileged group. As soon as she unlocked the door and turned on the lights, her cell phone rang. Jenna got excited; she immediately thought it was Carl calling to apologize. Maybe he realized just how cold he had acted toward her, and wanted to make it up to her. Jenna dropped her keys and her pocketbook on the desk, placed her bagel and coffee down and tried to answer her phone, but the call had already gone into voicemail. With excitement in her heart, she checked the message only to be disappointed by what she heard.

"Hi Jenna, this is Agatha. Listen, I was thinking about sending Courtney to New York with you next month. I think the show that Wilfred is planning would be good training for her. I had dinner with Courtney last night; and she is quite an investigative reporter, you should hear some of the tactics she used to track down her father. Courtney feels she is close to finding him; but I am not paying her to find her long lost father. I need her to stay focused. You know Millie Enterprises will be there and they always manage to beat us out of the best stories. With you and Courtney there, I'm sure we will have the best coverage possible. There is also a new journalist on the scene; his name is Barrington and he is very good. Try to meet him if you can. Call me back so we can discuss this in greater detail."

Jenna took a deep breath before playing the message again. This was so unlike Agatha to get that involved in an employee's personal life. Agatha was one of the most competitive bosses she ever worked for; she could not believe her boss would allow herself to be sidetracked by Courtney's ongoing family drama. The only thing Jenna found more disturbing than the bond that appeared to be developing between Agatha and Courtney was the fact that Agatha believed Courtney could help her cover Wilfred's show. Every well-known designer Jenna knew wanted to showcase their product in Wilfred's show, and the only reason Agatha's magazine was invited, was because of her friendship with Wilfred. Did Agatha really expect her to share the spotlight with Courtney? Jenna knew she could not say no to Agatha; in fact her boss rarely called her and when she did, it was usually because Agatha had already made up her mind about something. The phone call was just Agatha's way of informing Jenna of what she was ordering her to do. Jenna thought for a few minutes and instead of returning Agatha's call; she fumbled through her twelve inch rolodex and located Courtney's number. Courtney's phone rang several times, before going into voicemail and Jenna wondered if anyone ever answered their phones anymore.

"Courtney, this is Jenna. I just heard from Agatha and it seems she is a little concerned about your ability to do your job. It seems like you are constantly distracted with your attempts to find your father. Courtney, I am only telling you this because I want to help you. Agatha's magazine is a very upscale publication and as you know, there is a lot of competition out there. You need to shape up. Now, Agatha wants you to attend a very big showcase with me in New York. Personally, I don't believe you are ready for this type of assignment, but Agatha is the boss. If you want to keep your job, you need to be focused. I want to meet with you first thing in the morning. I will have my secretary call you to arrange a time; please make sure you are available; oh, and one more thing Courtney, you should really consider taking those braids out of your hair; it really does not fit the image of this company."

Jenna hung up the phone; she was not at all worried about any backlash from Agatha. It all made sense to her now. Jenna had worked for Agatha for twelve years and they knew each other all too well. Agatha had dinner with Courtney because she was concerned about Courtney's ability to handle her job; if Agatha was interested in keeping Courtney on board, she would have been direct in giving her a warning about her performance, but Agatha wanted Courtney gone and she was setting Jenna up to do it. Jenna knew the signs; she had been through this several times before. Each time a new writer was borderline, Agatha placed them under Jenna and within two or three months, they would quit. Jenna would continue to be the hard nose, editor no one wanted to work with and Agatha could be the innocent boss, who just happened to be caught in the middle.

Courtney dried her eyes as she watched the criminal activity from her hotel window. There was a church nearby and she wanted to stop in and see if anyone there knew anything about her father, but now after listening to Jenna's message she realized those plans would have to wait. With her job now on the line, Courtney had to regroup. The thought of spending another night in this crime infested neighborhood was too much for her, so she decided to drive across town and look for an apartment. As much as she wanted to find her father, she wanted success much more. After growing up in foster care, Courtney promised herself that one day she would have it all; beautiful clothes, expensive shoes, a big house and lots of money and she was determined not to let anything or anyone stop her.

Courtney got dressed, mapped out some directions and addresses to put into her GPS, and was ready to walk out the door when she remembered something she forgot to do. She went into the bathroom, reached for a pair of scissors and began cutting the long beautiful braids out of her hair. As she worked through the many rows of braids, she heard that familiar whisper, *for what does it profit a man to gain the whole world and forfeit his soul? Mark 8:36*

Courtney was not bothered by the whisper; she had been hearing it for years. She believed it was her imagination, her own thoughts or maybe even her own guilt for wanting all the world had to offer. The world taught her a lot, but it never taught her there would be times when God would speak to her, so she dismissed His voice, just as she had many times before.

CHAPTER FIVE

Mike rushed to get dressed and away from his wife. "I am not getting into this with you again, Rena. Give it a rest, will you?"

"I will not!" she screamed. "Where were you Friday night? Do you know how embarrassing it is to have my husband show up hours late to my birthday party? It was your job to host my party, not Carl's."

"Rena, we have been arguing about this for two days already; I told you I was on a case and got held up. I planned the party and it turned out nice and you're still not happy."

Rena stared at her husband then said, "You just don't get it, Mike. This is not about the party at all. It was my birthday, and all I really wanted was for you to put me first. I wanted you to make the time to be with me. I feel like you go out of your way to avoid being with me. What is it, Mike? Are you not happy with me? Just tell me!"

Mike stood up and slammed both hands against the wall. "It's that right there, Rena! Your pathetic way of making yourself the victim every time things don't go your way. You're angry all the time, and I'm sick and tired of trying to make you happy. You want the truth? Well, here it is. Most of the time I can't stand to be around you, and yes, there are many nights I don't want to come home! There, I said it. Are you happy now?"

Mike turned away from her and stormed out of the house and headed for the safety of his jeep. Rena did not bother to chase after him, the engine had started, and she could already hear him as he sped out of the driveway. Rena ran upstairs to the bedroom and flung the door open; her eyes locked in on Mike's customized book shelf; she knew his book collection meant the world to him, so she grabbed one section of his old war stories collection and began throwing them around the room; then she moved over to his home remodeling and self-help for home owner's books, and flung them around as well. Rena had always resented that book shelf. Mike refused to give her fifteen hundred dollars to start her catering business but he did not hesitate to spend over three thousand dollars on his bookshelf.

"With all of these self-help books you managed to collect, you couldn't find one to show you how to be a better husband? Do you know how much I hate you Mike? You have made my life miserable! You're not a good man; you're a liar and a cheat; and I will never, ever, forgive you for being with Desiree! All these humanitarian awards you received mean nothing! I wish people knew how you were at home, and how many times I had to resist telling people that their superhero can't even impregnate his wife. You may be an outstanding detective, but you are a lousy husband. You may be active in the community, but you are inactive at home." Rena was surprised at how easily the words she thought were safely hidden in her heart flew out of her mouth. Fifteen more minutes went by where Rena lost control in the privacy of her home. Finally, when she was done, she took a hot shower, put on her makeup, and sat on the edge of her bed. For one brief moment, she regretted the words she had spoken, but she convinced herself there was no harm done since no one heard her. Her mother always said, "What the world doesn't see doesn't count."

Looking over on her dresser, she noticed the time on the clock. It was nearly eleven o'clock, and her favorite cooking show was about to start. Rena felt an invisible bond with the two ladies who hosted the show; they were funny and cheerful and brought much needed joy into her mornings. Rena pressed through the channels and was relieved to find the show had not started yet, so she went into the kitchen and made herself a cup of tea. When she returned, she found the two hosts engaged in laugher.

Rena sat down on the bed, wondering what she had missed, when one of the hosts of the television show looked directly into the camera and with the laughter still in her voice she pointed and said, "For those of you just tuning in, there is still time to respond to today's question. 'What are you doing in secret that only you and God know about?'"

Rena sighed then responded, "I wish one day they would say something that actually pertained to me."

CHAPTER SIX

Desiree had a strong desire to be in church this evening. As Gabriel lay in his crib, she began getting ready for the seven o'clock service. A knock on the door startled her and she carefully walked to the door and checked the peephole. There were two people she did not want to see, Romeo was the first and Mr. Dave was the second.

"Come on, Ms. Hunter, open the door. We need to talk," Mr. Dave said.

Desiree unlocked the door and opened it. "I'm sorry, Mr. Dave, I know I'm late again, but I will have the rent for you, I promise. I just need to ask my parents for a little extra money."

Mr. Dave was not a big man but he was very intimidating. Desiree knew he only tolerated her lateness with the rent because of the baby. "Look, Ms. Hunter, we go through this every month, I can't keep letting you get away with paying late when all of my other tenants have to pay on time. I'm giving you until nine o'clock tonight. You need to have the full rent otherwise I have to put you out." As Mr. Dave limped away, Desiree gently closed the door and sat down on the bed. The last two weeks had been tough. Saturdays at the market were very busy, but it provided her with the extra money she needed to make the rent, but when her mother did not show up to watch her son, she had no choice but to stay home. To make matters worse, she ran out of milk and food for the week and had to dip into her rent money; now she found herself two hundred and six dollars short for the rent. Taking a deep breath, she picked up the phone and called her mother. Desiree was surprised her mom answered so quickly.

"Hello, Desiree," her mother said in a dry and somber tone.

"Mom, are you okay?"

"No, honey. I have a terrible headache, and your father is in a bad mood again." There was a long pause.

"Do you need me to come over or send help, Mom?"

"I'm okay, Desiree, but your father is coming. I have to go. Can we talk later?"

"Well, actually, Mom I need..."

"I'm Sorry, Desiree. I really have to go. Your father is calling me."

Desiree felt drained. Now instead of worrying about her rent, she was worried about her mother; she dropped to her knees and prayed. "Please God, watch over my mother and help her find safety. Please God. Amen."

Desiree woke Gabriel and got him ready for church. Just as she was preparing to leave, she realized Mr. Dave was still outside her door, talking to one of the tenants; she waited patiently as Mr. Dave said goodnight to the tenant, but instead of leaving Mr. Dave stood right outside her door, simply watching the traffic go by. Desiree became anxious; without her mother's help, she knew she would not have the rent money by nine o'clock, but she was not ready to confess that to Mr. Dave. The only other way out of her apartment was through the window in the bedroom, but that window led to the back alley; where it was dark and isolated, so she quickly dismissed that option. With only a few minutes left to get to church, she called out to God. "Lord, I know this may seem inpatient of me, but I really need to get out of here; can you please move Mr. Dave so I can get to church? Please, God, he's holding me up!"

Another fifteen minutes went by and Desiree continued looking through the peephole, only to find Mr. Dave was still blocking her path. Frustrated at having to wait, she cried out again, "Please, God, it's not like I want to go to the mall or anything. I'm trying to get to church!" Another ten minutes went by, and Mr. Dave was still outside. This was so unlike Mr. Dave who only seemed to come outside during rent time. Desiree sat on the futon and cried; she was frustrated and a bit angry. She knew God heard her prayers, but she couldn't understand why He would not move Mr. Dave.

Just a few feet away sat a frustrated Romeo. He was parked right outside Desiree's building and could see both her front entrance and her back window. Romeo was breathing heavily, and his patience was growing thin. He was all set to go in and take his revenge on Desiree when Mr. Dave appeared out of nowhere. In the two years he lived with Desiree, he never knew Mr. Dave to make his rounds at night to collect the rent; that was always something he did during the day.

Romeo slowly pulled the gun from his jacket and placed it into the glove compartment; he could not believe his luck. In just a short time he was able to steal a car and drive twenty miles without a license or insurance only to arrive to Desiree's building and have his path blocked by Mr. Dave. It did not matter that Mr. Dave was an old man; he was from the streets and Romeo did not care to test him. Angry, tired, and frustrated, Romeo decided he would let Desiree live one more night, then he would be back for her, and next time he would come prepared to take on Mr. Dave if he had to.

Desiree thought Mr. Dave would never leave, but eventually he did; she wrapped her son in a blanket and headed out the door. It was a long walk to the church but the cool air felt good and helped her to relax, but after a few minutes, Gabriel began to weigh her down. He had outgrown the flimsy stroller she managed to buy him a few months ago and with money being so tight, she still did not have enough saved up to get him a new stroller. In spite of the long walk, Desiree was not discouraged; she always felt rejuvenated after attending church, so she continued carrying her son the full nine blocks to church.

The evening service was uplifting, and Desiree felt encouraged. As the church began to clear out, she thought about calling her mother and asking if she and the baby could sleep there tonight. Anything was better than giving Mr. Dave another excuse. Desiree was so distracted by her thoughts that she did not see Carl walk up to her. "Hello, Desiree" he said in an upbeat voice. Carl reached for Gabriel, and to her surprise her son leaped into his arms.

"Wow, he never does that! I think he really likes you, Carl."

"Of course he does," replied Carl. "Uncle Carl is cool, right, little man?"

Gabriel then motioned for Carl to return him to his mother. By now Pastor Lee had made his way through the crowd and came over to speak to them. "Good evening, Carl. Desiree, it's always good to see you and Gabriel." Desiree smiled as she watched Pastor Lee attempt to pick Gabriel up, but Gabriel protested and reached for Carl instead. Pastor Lee smiled at him.

"Well, then I guess you don't want the books inside this envelope, do you, Gabriel?" Gabriel's eyes focused on the big colorful envelope, and then he reached out and made several attempts to grab it. "Desiree, do you and Gabriel have a ride home?"

Desiree knew better than to lie to him. "No, Pastor, we walked here." Pastor Lee looked over at Carl before responding to her. "Well, you know we can't let you walk home this time of night alone."

As he spoke, Pastor Lee threw another quick glance at Carl, who replied, "No sir, we would never let that happen. I'll see to it that they get home."

Pastor Lee patted Carl on the back. "Thank you, Carl. I'll ask Ms. Katherine for a car seat."

The ride home was stressful for Desiree, but she managed to hold up her end of the conversation with Carl. As soon as they pulled up to her building, Desiree noticed the time and became anxious.

"What's wrong?" asked Carl as Desiree hurried out of the car. She only had thirty minutes left before Mr. Dave would return, looking for the rent. As she watched Carl unbuckle her son from his seat, she contemplated asking him for the money, but Carl was a man, and men never did anything for women without expecting something in return. Desiree tried to fight back the tears, but her frustration was building, and the tears seemed to burst out on their own. Carl quickly walked over to her. "Desiree, what's wrong?"

"I'm okay. I just needed to talk to my mom, but she's not answering her phone."

"Well, if it's that serious I can take you over there."

"No, it's okay. I can just call her in the morning."

Carl studied Desiree briefly; he knew she was not telling him the truth. "Desiree, are you sure you don't want me to take you to see your mother? I can't just leave you here while you're upset."

Desiree wiped her face and managed to smile. Carl was always so kind to her, and she was glad she did not ask him for the money. The last thing she wanted was for Carl to think she was taking advantage of his kindness. "I'm okay, Carl. It's just mother and daughter stuff. I'm sure we will both be okay in the morning." Carl handed Gabriel to her. "Thanks for the ride home Carl."

"No problem Desiree; just let me walk you to the door, I need to be sure you are safely inside before I take off."

As soon as Carl left, she locked the door and put her son down on the futon. Gabriel immediately began crying for his milk. Desiree went into the kitchen and hoped she had enough milk left to feed her child. When she returned, she placed the cup of milk in Gabriel's hand, and Gabriel gave her his envelope to hold. Desiree decided to let him have the books inside; at least she could keep him quiet while she talked to Mr. Dave. As she opened the envelope and shook the contents loose, out dropped several small books, a toy and a set of bills totaling two hundred and six dollars.

CHAPTER SEVEN

Jenna was sitting at the traffic light, and steadily pressing on her horn. "Come on, lady, let's go!" The car ahead of her pulled off slowly, and that irritated Jenna even more, so she sped up in front of the driver and purposely cut her off. The woman driving yelled out at Jenna, saying she had her children in the car and asking if their lives were worth the two seconds she saved by cutting her off, but Jenna never heard a word of it. With her speed now up to eighty-three miles per hour, she was determined to make her appointment on time. Seconds later, without warning, her car began to slow down. Jenna looked at her dashboard and noticed the needle was past the "E" mark and the gas light was glowing. Jay had borrowed her car the night before and as usual returned it with an empty tank. Jenna managed to get her car onto the shoulder of the highway, then began yelling and cursing while pounding on the steering wheel. Pulling her expensive pocketbook from the passenger's seat; she searched for her cell phone and quickly called roadside service, but the customer service department was busy and it took her eight minutes to reach a live operator. "This is road service, how may we assist you?" The operator was warm and friendly, but as soon as Jenna began screaming insults at her, she hung up. Jenna waited a few minutes, and then called back;

this time she spoke to a different operator who assured her help was on the way. Still in a rage, Jenna dialed her sister's number, and Jay answered immediately.

"Jay!" Jenna shouted. "What's wrong with you? How could you return my car with an empty tank and not say a word? You are the most selfish person I know. Just wait until you ask me for another favor." As Jenna's voice echoed in Jay's ear, Jay turned up the volume on her headphones. "Where are you?" yelled Jenna.

"I'm in the car with Luther; we are on our way to sample cakes for the wedding." Jay's voice was even toned and showed no sign of concern for her sister's anger; when Jenna finished yelling, Jay simply hung up.

"What's wrong with your sister now?" asked Luther.

"She's upset because I didn't return the car with gas in it. Jenna is so bossy and she expects people to read her mind. If she wanted me to put gas back in her car, she should have said so." Jay removed her headphones, pushed her seat back and closed her eyes. "I hope they make good red velvet cake; I really don't want plain cake for the wedding. Red velvet cake would be nice."

It only took road service thirty minutes to get Jenna back on the road and she was relieved to know there was still time for her to make her appointment. As she merged back onto the highway, her cell phone rang; when she saw it was Rena, she answered, "Hey, Rena, I tried calling you a couple of times. I wanted to let you know how much I enjoyed the party, but I kept getting your voicemail."

"I know things have been crazy," replied Rena. "Mike and I are at it again. I can't stand my husband, but that's not why I'm calling. I want you to get Desiree's bags into a showcase."

"Rena, I told you before, she's not ready for the clientele I work with. Desiree's bags may do well in a swap meet, but they will never make it to Fifth Avenue."

"That's not true; you liked the bags before you realized Desiree made them."

"Look, I'm on my way to an interview right now. Let me talk to some people and see what I can do. I'll call you back later." Jenna hung up, knowing she had no intention of helping Rena or Desiree. There were tons of designers with real talent who could not get their products into showcases; the competition was fierce, and without money or connections there was no way Desiree could break into this industry.

When Jenna arrived at her destination, she pulled into a priority parking space and sat quietly for several minutes. This was a major assignment for her, and she needed to organize her thoughts, but the only thoughts that came to mind were of Carl. No matter how hard she tried, she could not forget him. The university was only ten minutes away, and his classes would be ending soon. Jenna had to find a way to get back into Carl's arms; she already had plans to invite him to go on vacation with her, and she also wanted him to escort her to Jay's wedding. Her younger sister getting married was an event she did not look forward to, but with Carl in her life she could handle anything.

Jenna reached into her purse and pulled out her lipstick and foundation. After taking a minute to admire herself in the mirror, she threw the items back into her purse, shoved her designer shades onto her face, and headed to her interview. Jenna decided she was not done with Carl yet. As soon as she finished her interview, she would drive up to the university and pay Carl a visit. If he fell for her once, she was certain she could make him fall for her a second time.

Carl sat in the college lounge reviewing material with a few of his colleagues. After a couple of hours the lounge emptied out, and Carl prepared to leave.

As he made his way to the parking lot, he wished he had something or someone to go home to. Wondering what he would do about dinner, he unlocked his car, tossed his briefcase in the back seat, and slipped inside. Carl roamed through his selection of music and placed a CD inside the player, then started the car. As soon as he drove off, his cell phone rang. Carl looked at the caller ID and was surprised to see "Jenna Livingston" boldly displayed across the screen. He continued to drive as the phone rang several more times. Despite not having any plans for the evening, he was still not interested in wasting any more time with her. When his message tone beeped, Carl was surprised; he could not imagine what Jenna would have to say to him, but he was curious and decided to pull over and check the message. "Hello, Carl, this is Jenna. Listen, I just wanted to apologize for last week. I know it was rude of me to show up at your home the way I did. I can understand you not wanting to talk to me, but I am in the area and thought we could meet for a quick drink; if nothing else, I owe you an apology." Carl was very surprised by Jenna's message. Jenna apologizing was the last thing he expected to hear. After playing the message a second time, he decided a quick drink with Jenna was better than an evening alone, so he called her back and after a brief conversation, agreed to meet her for a drink.

The restaurant was only a few blocks away, and Carl arrived first. He pushed his seat back and continued to listen to his music while he waited for Jenna. As he waited, he began to have second thoughts about seeing Jenna again; he felt foolish for agreeing to meet a woman who was mean and nasty and who showed up to his home unannounced and acting like a crazy woman. Just as he considered backing out of the date, he saw the familiar Silver Volvo enter the parking lot. Carl watched closely as Jenna emerged from the car wearing gray shoes, a light-blue dress with a gray and silver scarf that was elegantly thrown around her shoulders. Jenna strolled through the parking lot with the same level of confidence she had when she first entered his home. Jenna did not notice Carl as she walked right past him sitting in his car. With Jenna now in his full view, he quickly sat up, and his eyes followed her every move. Suddenly, his evening was looking better, and he rushed out of the car to greet her. "Hello, Jenna."

"Oh, Carl, I thought you were already inside." Carl moved quickly toward the door and held it open for her. "Thank you, sir," she teased as she flung her scarf over her shoulder and walked inside.

The waiter escorted them to a table, where they were handed a menu for appetizers and drinks only. Carl had never been to this restaurant before, and he was quite impressed with Jenna's selection. The décor of the restaurant was eclectic, with most of the modern artwork matched to artwork from the Roman periods. They both ordered drinks and kept the conversation light. An hour later, the aroma coming from the kitchen tempted Carl into ordering a Western dish that he happily shared with Jenna.

Three more hours went by, while Carl and Jenna ate, drank, and amused themselves with Jenna spoon feeding Carl his dessert.

When they finally decided to leave, Jenna held onto Carl's arm as he escorted her to her car. He wrapped Jenna's scarf around her shoulders and kissed her.

"I hope that wasn't a goodbye kiss," she said.

"No Jenna, that was a forget-me-not kiss," he said

and laughed. "Don't forget, we have a date next Saturday."

"I'll rush right home and mark my calendar," she replied as she ran her two fingers across his lips, wiping away any traces of her lipstick. Carl took her car keys, opened the door, and waited for her to get inside. "Drive safely, Jenna, and call me the minute you get home so I know you made it home safely."

Jenna pulled her scarf off of her shoulders and smiled at him. "I'll be fine," she said while attempting to close her door, but Carl held the car door open.

"I didn't ask you if you would be fine. I asked you to call me and let me know you got home safely."

Jenna blushed and said, "Okay, I'll call. Just be sure to wait up for me."

Carl walked to his car and started to drive home. He knew Jenna was not the woman for him, but he hoped, he would be able to change her.

Jenna's call came just as Carl was pulling into his driveway.

"I'm home Carl, safe and sound."

"Well, you might be safe, but the jury is still out on how sound you are," he replied.

Jenna laughed. "Okay, I may have had that coming. I feel terrible about the way I acted, Carl."

"Don't worry about it, Jenna. We decided to start over, so let's just focus on our plans for next weekend. If we start out early enough, we can see all of the exhibits we talked about and then have a late dinner."

"I'm looking forward to seeing you again, Carl, and thank you again for dinner. I know we were only meeting for drinks, but I'm glad you stayed longer."

"Well, I enjoyed your company, Jenna, and thank you for sharing your dessert with me; it tasted much better having it fed to me."

Jenna laughed. "I guess you can tell I need someone to take care of. Would you mind if that someone were you?"

Carl was now smiling. "Do you think you could take care of me?"

Jenna responded in a soft voice. "I know I can."

"Okay, then the job is yours," he replied. "Good night, Miss Jenna."

"Good night, Mr. Dupree. Enjoy the rest of your weekend."

Jenna was thrilled, not only did she congratulate herself on winning Carl back, but she now began to see herself planning her own wedding.

Maurice broke her heart, but Carl was going to make everything better. Unlike Maurice, Carl was very well educated, handsome and successful. Maurice was good looking but he was also broke and he used her like an ATM machine until she was out of funds. But Carl did not need her money. Judging from the artwork that hung on the walls of his million dollar home, it was clear that Carl had an abundance of disposable income.

CHAPTER EIGHT

The morning was cold and damp. Pastor Lee was in his office preparing for the morning service, he smiled when Katherine Johnson came in. Katherine was his best friend and his best line of support. "Are you ready, Lee?"

"I'm as ready as I will ever be," he replied.

Katherine sat down next to him. "I know your testimony will help a lot of people, but most of all it will help you, and don't worry, Lee. I will be close by if you need me."

Pastor Lee smiled at her. "I always need you, Katherine."

Several minutes later, Pastor Lee entered the pulpit and greeted his congregation. "Today, I would like to take a few minutes to share my personal testimony with you. I believe my testimony will help many of you with some of the issues and challenges you all are facing.

About twenty years ago, I was living what the world would consider to be the American Dream. I was an executive in a major corporation, earning a six-figure salary. I had a beautiful wife and a daughter named Courtney. We lived in a five-bedroom home, and we had a very large bank account. I played golf with the CEO, attended parties hosted by my boss, and enjoyed all of the privileges a high-level employee was granted. Then one day a meeting took place behind closed doors, and with one stroke of the pen my boss wiped out my entire future. I was thanked for twenty five years of service before being escorted out of the building. I never saw it coming, and I left work that day a stunned and broken man.

"I tried for more than a year to find another job that would allow me to maintain my lifestyle, but after eighteen months of feeling like a failure, I began taking a drink here and there to ease my pain. Eventually, I allowed the drinking to comfort me; I found it easier to turn my grief over to the bottle than to deal with the constant rejections. Before I knew it, my drinking was wrecking my marriage. I would go on drinking binges for days, knowing when I came home, my wife would simply pray and ask the Lord to help me. Then one night I ran into some of my drinking buddies, and they took me to an event with an open bar. I spent the whole night enjoying all the free liquor I could handle; I never calculated what it would end up costing me in the end.

The next morning my wife and daughter were out food shopping. Having the house to myself, I decided to sneak in a few more drinks before they came back home. Several hours later there was a knock on my door. Two police officers stood there and told me my family had been in a car accident. I was shocked. All I could do was stand there in disbelief, dazed and filthy drunk, barely understanding them as they tried to omit the harsh details of my wife's car accident."

Pastor Lee's voice grew shaky, and tears were now streaming down his face. The congregation sat silently still; many of them had heard about the car accident that claimed the life of his wife, but no one knew all of the details. "A drunk driver in a dusty blue Chevy was traveling at a very high speed and ran into my wife's car.

A couple of people managed to pull my daughter Courtney out of the car, but they could not free my wife. When the drunk driver realized he had hit them, he got out of his car to help. I was told he kept asking if everyone was okay, but then he got scared and stumbled back to his car. Witnesses said the drunk driver must have thought he was pulling off, but instead he put the car in reverse, and sped backwards at full speed; the car was aimed right at my daughter. There was a doctor who witnessed the accident and he was trying to help my wife; when he saw the car heading for Courtney, he ran over and threw himself over Courtney and saved her life.

A few hours later, the police brought me to the hospital. My wife passed away but my daughter and the doctor recovered. I wanted to be with my daughter, but because I was intoxicated, I was only able to spend a little time with her. With no family in the area, my daughter Courtney was placed in emergency foster care, because I was deemed unfit to care for her. I begged everyone I knew to help me get her back. Most of the people I called on for help would not even return my calls. Then one day I met a young attorney by the name of James Marshall, who was not afraid to tell me my daughter Courtney would be better off living with strangers than to be raised by a father who was a drunk."

Pastor Lee looked down at James Marshall and smiled, then he said to the congregation, "James Marshall and I have been friends ever since. That was my wakeup call, but unfortunately it took me several more years before I could sober up. My daughter was eventually adopted, and as many of you know, I have never been able to find her.

Today is Courtney's birthday and I can stand before you and smile as I remember telling God how I begged so many people for help. I reached out to the courts, the therapists, lawyers, caseworkers, and even the judge; but no one was willing to help me. At that very moment, I sat down to watch television, and a young pastor was being interviewed, and he told how he waited for nine years for someone to help him out of a situation and kept complaining to God that no one would help him. He then said God asked him, 'Why didn't you ask me?' His testimony helped me realize, I had never asked God for his help. I don't know why my daughter has not attempted to find me, but I do know only God can touch her heart and bring her back to me.

"One of the biggest mistakes I ever made was believing I was only a good man as long as I had my job; I trusted in my corporate position, and when that position failed me, I believed I had no self-worth. I realize now, that my boss did not end my future, because my future was never in my boss's hands to begin with."

When the service ended, Katherine Johnson went into Pastor Lee's office and closed the door. Pastor Lee sat with tears in his eyes, but they were tears he would only allow Katherine to see.

"Something is different this time Katherine. I know God is moving and Courtney is coming back to me."

Katherine walked over to the conference table and began clearing off the papers that were left from an earlier meeting. She would do anything for him, but she could not stand to watch his heart break every time he believed this was the year his daughter was coming back.

Pastor Lee watched Katherine for several minutes. He knew she was avoiding any talk about Courtney coming home. Every year on Courtney's birthday, his heart broke, knowing his daughter was out there somewhere. Pastor Lee suffered each year on this day; and Katherine suffered right along with him.

"Katherine, I know you think I'm being emotional,

again, but Courtney's presence is strong this time. I can't explain it, but it seems like she is close by. I know God is moving Katherine and He is leading her back to me!"

Katherine continued clearing off the table. When she realized he was waiting for a response, she smiled and said, "If you believe in your heart, that God is bringing Courtney back, then I stand in agreement with you Lee."

CHAPTER NINE

M̲ike sat quietly at the kitchen table reading his newspaper; he knew Rena was upset with him, but he decided to ignore it. She knew his work kept him busy, and instead of supporting him, all she did was complain. "Mike, you know it would be nice if you made me a priority for once. You said you were taking the day off, and now you're going into work. I can't believe you."

Mike stood up and poured his coffee down the sink. "You know, Rena, you should really find something productive to do with your life; a job would be nice." Rena turned toward him, but before she could respond, he was out the door.

Mike's comments cut her deeply, and if he thought he would escape her that easily, he had another thing coming. Rena picked up her cell phone and started to call him, but there was a knock on the door. "Maybe Mike forgot his key," she thought as she rushed to the door and snatched it open. Standing there with a cake in her hands was Katherine Johnson. "Oh, good morning, Miss Katherine, is everything okay?"

"I should be asking you that question, Rena; your husband nearly ran me over."

"I'm sorry about that, Miss Katherine; we had a little disagreement this morning. Please come in."

Miss Johnson stepped inside. "Rena, did you forget

we were supposed to go over the menu for next month's dedication ceremony this morning? I was hoping we could finalize the menu and get it to the printer today."

"I'm sorry, Miss Katherine, I did forget, but that's okay, we can work on it now. I'll make some coffee and we can get started."

Miss Katherine sat down at the table and carefully asked, "Have you given any thought to going to talk to Pastor Lee about the trouble you and Mike are having?"

Rena brought two cups of coffee over and placed them on the table. "Miss Katherine, Mike and I have to work this out ourselves; besides I'm sure Mike doesn't want everyone in our business."

"Is it Mike who has too much pride to ask for help, or is it you?" Rena did not respond; she kept stirring her coffee slowly while contemplating whether or not she wanted to talk about her troubled marriage. Katherine Johnson looked at Rena, then she got up, and without saying a word she pulled Rena out of her chair and hugged her.

"Miss Katherine, your hugs are like instant medicine," said Rena as she allowed herself to be lost in the warmth and comfort of Miss Katherine's arms.

Miss Katherine gently pushed Rena away from her and pulled out a chair. "Sit down, Rena. I want to talk to you. Now I am not one to interfere in the lives of young married people, but I love you and Mike, and it's not hard to see that the two of you are in trouble."

"We argue all the time, Miss Katherine, and it's getting worse. Mike wants me to get a job, but I want to start my own catering company. I only need about fifteen hundred dollars to get started, but Mike keeps saying no. He works all of the time, and lately he seems to be doing it just to avoid coming home."

"I see; and what about you, Rena? What is your

contribution to this problem?" Rena was stunned; she expected sympathy from Miss Katherine, but clearly Miss Katherine was blaming her. "Honey, if you make your home a battlefield, your husband will continue to avoid it." Miss Katherine held Rena's chin in her hands. "Choose your words carefully, Rena. Each time you open your mouth up against your husband, you give the enemy access into your marriage and once the enemy gets in, he will destroy everything. Now, you married a man who loves God, and you can't do any better than that. Let God deal with Mike, while you focus on what God has called you to do."

"I know you're right, Miss Katherine."

"Of course I'm right," replied Miss Katherine. "Now I have to get going, we can work on the menu another time, but remember, Rena, I'm here if you need me."

"We always need you, Miss Katherine." Rena gave Miss Katherine another hug before escorting her to the door. Rena then spent the next few hours cleaning the house and cooking Mike's favorite meal. By seven o'clock that evening, their home was filled with the aroma of jerk chicken, macaroni and cheese, homemade buttermilk biscuits, and sweet corn. Rena lit candles throughout the living room and put on a form-fitting red dress that Mike loved seeing her in; she was so excited, she could not wait until Mike came home.

By nine o'clock, Rena was growing restless. Mike had not come home, and she realized he had not called her all day. Resentment began creeping in, and Rena was convinced Mike was avoiding coming home again. After several of her calls went into his voicemail, she changed her clothes, grabbed her car keys, and headed out the door. This time, when Mike decided to come home, he would see what an empty house felt like.

As she settled into her jeep, she had a dreadful

feeling; it was as if something was telling her not to go, but she ignored it. Rena buckled herself in and sped out of the driveway and onto the dark road. It had just started to rain, and the night air was cool. Rena hated nights like this; they made everything seem so bleak. As she sped down the dark street, she did not see the car quickly approaching her. The driver frantically blew his horn, and Rena quickly got back in her lane. When the car passed her, she realized she did not have her lights on. Desiree's apartment was still more than thirty minutes away, and that feeling of dread was now in the pit of her stomach, but once again she ignored it and continued to drive.

Finally, she made it to Desiree's apartment. Rena took a deep breath and sat quietly for a few minutes. Between the dark and wet roads and the dizziness that started to overwhelm her, she wasn't sure she would make it. When she saw the light on in Desiree's apartment, she began to feel better. Although Desiree was only twenty-four years old, Rena found her to be quite comforting to talk to. Desiree never spoke badly of Mike; she simply provided a safe place for Rena to vent. That was one of the things Rena loved about Desiree, she had a kind heart and always tried to see the best in people. As Rena sat in her truck, she recalled the many nights she took care of Desiree whenever Mrs. Hunter had to be hospitalized due to her husband's abuse. Rena's parents always took Desiree in, but she was the one who tucked Desiree in at night and told her she needed to pray. Rena never imagined it would be Desiree who would now give her that same advice.

The rain was still falling, so she grabbed a baseball cap from the backseat, locked the doors, and walked cautiously toward the building. Desiree lived in one of the most crime-ridden neighborhoods in Atlanta, and if

Mike knew she was here alone, he would be furious with her. As she approached the entrance of the building, she felt some of the men staring at her. Rena pulled her baseball cap down, trying to cover her eyes, and then she held her sweater closed tightly as she hurried past them. In order to get to Desiree's apartment, she had to go into the building, then down a flight of stairs that led to an alley. The alley was dark, and the stench of urine filled the air. Rena held her breath and knocked on the door; she looked around anxiously as she waited for a response. Minutes later Desiree opened the door and gave Rena a surprised look. "Are you busy?" Rena asked. Desiree knew something was wrong; Rena would never come to this neighborhood alone at night. Desiree gently pulled Rena inside; she could tell her friend had been crying. "I was just about to run out and get Gabriel some medicine; he has an ear infection and has been cranky all day."

"Oh, well, why don't you go, and I'll stay here with him?" offered Rena, but Desiree did not respond. Rena watched as Desiree placed a blanket over her sleeping son and kissed his forehead. Rena looked around the tiny basement apartment. It had a true basement feel; it was cold, dark, and dreary. Rena followed Desiree into the bedroom and saw that Gabriel was still sleeping in his tiny crib. Most two-year-old children would be in a toddler bed.

Desiree walked out to the living room, and Rena followed her, remaining silent until Desiree looked over at her, crossed her arms, and asked, "Okay, now what's up with you?"

"Nothing," Rena replied, trying to sound sincere. Desiree glanced over at the clock on the table, then back at Rena with a raised eyebrow and waited. "It's complicated, Dee. Why don't you run out and get the baby his medicine? I will fill you in on the details when you get back."

"Well, I guess I could make better time if I left him here. Are you sure you don't mind? I mean, this is not exactly the suburbs you know."

"I'll be fine," replied Rena.

"Okay then, I won't be long." Desiree struggled into her jacket and headed out the door.

"Bring back some chocolate!" shouted Rena. "Okay, I'll bring back something good!" replied Desiree.

Rena was glad she made the drive to come see Desiree. While her friends could not understand how she could forgive Desiree for sleeping with Mike, Rena understood it all too well. Mike was the college football star, very handsome, very popular and very much a ladies' man. Desiree, on the other hand was a frightened young girl, searching for the love she never received from her own father. It was easy for Desiree to be taken with Mike, but Mike was older, and he should have known better. Mike knew Desiree was like family to her and that caused Rena more pain than anything else Mike had ever done. Shortly after the one-night stand, Desiree and her mother again fled from their abusive home. Mike never denied what happened, and he never apologized for it either; and that caused Rena's resentment toward him to grow. In the six years Desiree was gone, so much had happened; Rena and Mike got married, and Rena heard that Desiree had given birth to a son and named him Gabriel, and now for reasons she herself was not quite sure of, Rena was ready to put the past behind her and restore her relationship with Desiree.

Rena put all the locks on the door, then went into the bedroom to check on Gabriel. The baby was asleep, but she could not resist the urge to see him again, so she tip toed into the room and over to his crib. Gabriel was a beautiful child; his skin was smooth and dark, and he had an abundance of curly black hair. Rena stood quietly over him, but when he began to stir, she stepped back and slowly backed out of the room. Rena hoped Desiree would not be gone too long; she really did not like being in the apartment alone and she was beginning to feel dizzy again. With only one small lamp on in the apartment, Rena decided she needed more light, so she walked over toward the light switch on the wall, reached up for the switch, and then she fell to the ground.

Romeo managed to get the car started. It had taken hours, but he was determined. Living on the streets taught him a lot about survival, and stealing cars was one of the first things he learned to do. Romeo drove slowly; it was crucial that he not attract any attention. The stolen car was bad enough, and he knew it was only a matter of time before the owners of the car reported it stolen. He did not care what happened to him in the end; getting Desiree back for having him locked up was all he cared about. Romeo's plan was to take Gabriel and make Desiree watch helplessly as he took her son away. He tapped his chest, making sure the knife was still in place. This time, if Mr. Dave was anywhere around, he would be the first victim and if Desiree tried to stop him, she would be the second.

Romeo slowly rolled the car into a parking space in front of Desiree's building, and with a sigh of relief, he turned off the engine and dimmed the lights. He could see the light on in her apartment and was relieved to know she was home. Looking around, he noticed Mr. Dave's old red pickup truck was gone. Convinced his plan would not be interrupted this time, Romeo was filled with excitement. He could not wait to see the look on Desiree's face when he confronted her. How dare she leave him, knowing what his own mother did to him? Didn't she remember how his mother had to choose between taking care of him or running off with her boyfriend? Didn't Desiree remember him telling her how he came home from school and found a note from his mother telling him to be good and to take care of himself? How was an eight-year-old kid supposed to take care of himself? Did his mother think the ten dollars she left him would last forever? Did she know that the neighborhood kids took the ten dollars as soon as they saw him with it? Desiree knew all of his pain, and she still walked out on him just because he roughed her up a few times; she was no different from his own mother. Filled with grief, anger, and despair, Romeo got out of the car and headed toward her building, carrying the knife in his pocket along with the scar he bore against women. In a few minutes, he intended to make Desiree pay for everything his mother had done to him.

Desiree lived alongside of a dark alley, which presented a perfect opportunity for him to get in and out of the apartment without being seen, but Romeo was not too concerned about witnesses; people in this neighborhood were not likely to call the police for assistance. In this neighborhood it was every man and woman for themselves.

Wearing black army boots and prepared for battle, Romeo walked confidently through the dark alley and went straight to the back bedroom window, flashing a cocky grin as he anticipated how easy this kidnapping was going to be. He tried the window and found it opened easily. Mr. Dave never fixed anything in this building. Romeo quietly pulled the window up and slipped in. He ignored the child sleeping in his crib and made his way to the door, and pressed his ear against it. Desiree could not be asleep so early, yet he heard no movement at all in the apartment. "Good enough," he thought. "When she hears her child crying, she will come running in, but it will be too late. I will have the kid in my hands and out the window before she can call for help." Romeo scanned the room; it was just as he remembered it, tiny and dark but clean. He made his way toward the crib; only this time instead of simply taking the child, his mind was instantly filled with more hideous thoughts aimed at the child. Romeo reached into the crib, but right before his hands could touch the child, he was met with an incredible force of light that blinded him. Romeo dropped to the floor trying desperately to bury his face into anything that would relieve him from this light; but it was to no avail, the light was too powerful, too intense and too blinding. The presence of this light caused his whole body to be filled with terror. Romeo grabbed the legs of the crib and tried desperately to call out for help but each time he opened his mouth, he could tell his lips were moving, but the words would not come out. As he lay trembling on the floor, he managed to release his grip from the legs of the crib, and within seconds the light was gone. Romeo stayed on the floor for several minutes unable to move. With tears streaming down his face and his heart pounding he looked around, desperately for someone to help him. Suddenly, the baby began to cry and he went into a state of panic; somehow he knew he would encounter that light again, unless he moved away from that baby. Romeo did not have the strength to walk, so he crawled toward the window and after several attempts, he was able to climb out.

The night air, helped him to breathe, something he struggled to do, while that light was present. Now, all he wanted to do was to get as far away from Desiree and that baby and never tell anyone what he experienced.

Romeo took a few steps past the window when a horrifying image caught his attention. There was a body lying on the living room floor. Romeo imagined it had to be Desiree; this would explain why she never came into the bedroom for her son. He moved closer to the window and saw that the body was lying perfectly still. His heart sank. Desiree appeared shorter, heavier, and much older than he remembered, but he had been gone a long time. Romeo was suddenly filled with grief; he hated Desiree, but she was the only person who ever loved him, and now she may be dead or dying. As much as he wanted to run away, he could not just leave her there, so he pulled out his stolen cell phone and made a call he never thought he would make. He tapped 911 on the key pad, and the operator answered immediately. "This is 911, what is your emergency?"

Desiree walked toward her building, nearly out of breath; her errands always took extra time since she had so far to walk. Holding the two chocolate cakes she had bought, her eyes suddenly caught sight of a familiar figure that put fear into her heart. It was Romeo! Desiree dropped the cakes and began screaming as she ran toward her apartment. Fearing that he may have harmed her baby, she began yelling. "Romeo! You better not have hurt my son!" As soon as Romeo saw Desiree, he took off running, but now he was confused; if Desiree was running toward him, then who was the woman lying on the floor? Did he make that 911 call for nothing? There was no time to worry about that; he needed to get away before Desiree could have him locked up again.

Desiree was at her front door, banging frantically while screaming for Rena to open the door. She could hear Gabriel crying, and it brought her some relief; as long as he cried, she knew he was still alive. Realizing Rena was not responding, she ran around to the back alley, climbed into the bedroom window and got her son. Desiree's hands were shaking as she prepared to open the bedroom door. Her heart warned her that she was about to see something terrible. Rena would never let Gabriel cry unless she was not able to get to him. Holding her son tightly, Desiree grabbed the bedroom door and flung it open; her eyes focused on Rena's body lying on the floor, and she screamed as she backed out of the living room. "Someone help me! Call the police," she begged. "Call an ambulance. Oh, please don't let her be dead!"

As soon as the paramedics arrived, they went straight to Rena; she was in a desperate state, and they struggled to find a pulse. A number of police officers were on the scene and they tried to calm Desiree down long enough to get the details on what happened. Desiree believed Romeo broke into her apartment and attacked Rena, and that was exactly how she reported the incident.

"He was after me," she cried. "Rena was just here watching the baby. Romeo attacked her, thinking it was me. It's my fault he hurt her. Is she going to be okay? Please tell me she's going to be okay."

The police officer ignored her plea. "Who is Romeo, Ma'am?"

"Officer, I need to know where they are taking her. I have to let her husband know what happened."

The officer taking the statement responded coldly, "Look, you can check on your friend later, but right now I need you to answer my questions." Desiree looked up at the heavyset officer with silver hair and a stern look. Her eyes followed him as he moved away from her and headed toward the window. "Did you leave this window open?"

Desiree ignored his question; instead, she replied in a soft and casual tone. "You need to contact Detective

Rollins."

The officer gave Desiree an annoying look and said, "Contact who?"

"Detective Rollins," replied Desiree. "That woman you don't seem too concerned about is his wife." With one eye still on Desiree, the officer spoke into his radio. "Sergeant, you'd better come in here. It's one of our own."

Mike arrived home shortly after nine o'clock, only to find Rena was not home. He called her mother and stopped by the church, but no one had seen her. Mike made another call to her cell phone, but she did not answer. Deep down inside, he knew something was wrong; his wife would not be out this time of night, and no matter how mad she was, she would always let him know where she was. As he drove, his thoughts were on Rena and how difficult things had been for them lately. All they seemed to do was argue and disappoint each other. Mike pulled into the parking lot of his station and was about to call Rena again when a call came over his radio, a domestic disturbance. "What else is new?" he thought, but as soon as the address was announced, Mike froze; he knew that address all too well. It was Desiree's apartment, and a domestic situation at that address could only mean one thing; Romeo was out of jail and had gone after Desiree again. Mike was certain that Rena was somehow caught up in Desiree's mess. He put the car in reverse, put on his lights and siren, and sped out of the parking lot. As he raced to Desiree's apartment, he made one last attempt to reach Rena on her cell phone and was relieved when he heard a voice answer, until he realized it was a man's voice answering his wife's phone. "Who is this?" demanded Mike.

"This is Officer Samuel, who am I speaking to?"

Mike took control. "This is Detective Rollins; why are

you answering my wife's phone?"

The officer fell silent, and Mike repeated his question. "Detective, you may want to get down here; there's been an incident. We are still sorting out the details." Mike hung up the phone. He refused to listen to anyone tell him something may have happened to Rena. As long as he didn't hear it, he didn't have to face the possibility; if anything happened in Desiree's apartment, let it be Desiree who got hurt and not his wife. Mike rushed through the streets and with his sirens blazing he dodged in and out of traffic. He just needed to see his wife and make sure she was okay, and then he would go after Romeo and deal with him privately. Mike's hands were cold as ice, and the adrenalin began to rush through his body. All he could think about was his wife and the fear Romeo must have put into her. Mike wanted Romeo so badly, he could already taste his blood, he knew when he found Romeo, he would kill him; he just needed to get to him before the police did.

The hospital was crawling with police, and Rena woke to find her husband surrounded by the police officers from his precinct. Mike looked tired and uneasy, and Rena knew something terrible had happened. Looking around her room, she tried to recall the events that led to her being hospitalized but she quickly became overwhelmed and cried out for Mike. As soon as he heard his wife's voice, Mike ran to her side. "Rena, honey, I'm so glad you're okay."

"Mike, what happened? Why am I in this hospital?"

Mike reached over and took her hand. "I don't want you to worry about any of this, Rena. I'm going to take care of everything."

"Take care of what, Mike? What happened to me?"

"Rena, you don't remember going to Desiree's apartment last night?"

"I want you to tell me what happened," she yelled.

Mike tried to answer her as carefully as possible. There was no need to go into details, when he himself was having trouble dealing with what he believed had happened. "My station is still sorting out the details, but it seems like Romeo was released from jail and went after Desiree again. My guess is she called you instead of calling the police." Mike looked at his wife, then asked, "Rena, why on earth would you go running over there like that?"

"Desiree didn't call me; she didn't even know I was coming over. Actually," Carl's entrance into the room interrupted Rena's explanation.

Mike walked away from Rena and rushed over to Carl. "Let's go outside where we can talk." Rena started to cry; she needed Mike to be there and explain to her what happened, but as usual he had other priorities.

When the doctor entered the room, Rena was still crying. "Why won't anyone tell me what happened to me?" she pleaded.

"I don't believe they know everything yet, Mrs. Rollins."

"But they know something," answered Rena.

"Mrs. Rollins, please try to stay calm. I spoke with your husband, and the police seem to have things under control. He is very worried about you, but I assured him there are no signs of a physical attack. I can't tell you anything more than that right now. Mrs. Rollins, I do need to ask you a few questions. Have you taken any medication in the past twenty-four hours?"

Rena felt drained and betrayed. Everyone wanted information on what happened to her, but no one was willing to share their information with her. The doctor studied her chart then he turned to her and waited. "I take medication for anxiety and high blood pressure; those are the only two pills I took. Doctor, if you don't mind, I am really tired, and I just want to be alone right now."

"That's fine, Mrs. Rollins; I have all the information I need for now."

As soon as the doctor left the room, Rena reached into her pocketbook and pulled out her cell phone. There was one person she knew would help her get the answers she so desperately needed. Rena glanced over at the clock on the wall; the time was 6:08 a.m. She hit the dial key on her cell phone, and on the sixth ring she heard a sleepy and dazed response. "Hello?"

"Cookie, it's me, Rena. I'm sorry to call you so early, but I am in the hospital."

"What! What happened? Are you okay?"

"I don't know what happened, Cookie. Mike is here, but he won't tell me anything. Can you please come to the hospital?" Cookie questioned Rena for several more minutes before agreeing to come to the hospital.

Cookie knew she was driving too fast, but she made it to the hospital in less than twenty minutes. She parked in the first spot she found, rushed inside and managed to squeeze herself into an already packed elevator. When the elevator doors opened, Cookie stepped off and walked boldly down the hall. Mike was only a few feet away from her, still talking to Carl. Cookie marched right in between the two men; never stopping, she simply held up a finger and announced, "I'll be back to talk to you in a few minutes. What room is Rena in?"

Mike pointed and replied, "That way, she's in room 211." Carl looked briefly at the woman. He remembered seeing her before, but could not recall where. Mike watched Cookie enter Rena's room, and then he turned to Carl, "I guess I better call Rena's parents before anyone else does. I'll be back in a minute." Carl was still not clear on what actually happened to Rena, but he could not blame Mike for being scattered. He stood in the hallway and waited patiently for Mike to return.

"Rena, what's going on? Are you okay?"

"I don't know anything, Cookie. The doctors and nurses keep asking me questions; the police are asking me questions, but no one will tell me how I ended up here and I'm scared."

Cookie threw her purse on the foot of the bed, then walked back to the door and peeked out. "There are cops all over this place. Did someone break into your house or something?"

"No, nothing like that" replied Rena.

Cookie continued to watch the activity in the hallway. "Isn't that Mike's friend, Carl? What's he doing here?"

Rena suddenly began to scream, causing Cookie to break her concentration.

"What happened to the baby and Desiree? I remember hearing Desiree screaming! Please, Cookie, please find out what happened to them." Rena was crying so hard she was struggling to catch her breath.

Cookie poured a glass of water and held it up to Rena's mouth. "Okay now Rena, just relax. Mike is right outside, let me go talk to him and see what I can find out. Maybe we can get Mike or Carl to go check on Desiree. Just calm down and let me handle this." Cookie's words brought the comfort Rena needed. Cookie said she would handle things, and that was all Rena needed to hear.

Carl was standing alone in the hallway when Cookie approached him. "Carl, we need to talk." Now Carl understood why he had not recognized Cookie before;

she was dressed conservatively. "I was just in with Rena, and she's worried about Desiree."

Carl took a step back and asked, "What about Desiree?"

"I don't know, but Rena seems to think she may have been hurt or something."

Carl turned away from her and ran up to Mike. "What happened to Desiree and the baby?"

Mike had just finished talking to Rena's parents; his reply to Carl was dry and unconcerned. "The officers were able to get a statement from her. Apparently, she was just returning home from the store and saw Romeo running away from the building. Desiree said she ran inside to get the baby and found Rena lying on the floor; the baby's fine. They don't know who called the police, but the paramedics said if they had arrived three minutes later, it would have been too late to save Rena."

Carl let the information sink in, then asked, "Did anyone call Desiree's mom or Miss Katherine to stay with her?"

Mike became irritated. "How should I know?"

"I have to go check on them," replied Carl. "I'll be back as soon as I can."

"No! I need you here looking after Rena," ordered Mike.

"Come on, Mike, Romeo is not stupid enough to walk into this hospital and go after Rena; besides, he's probably someplace hiding out by now."

Mike moved up close to Carl and was now in his face. "I didn't call you down here to check on Desiree. Romeo attacked my wife, and I need to handle that!"

"You don't know that," replied Carl.

"Well, then let me tell you what I do know. I know my wife is lying in that hospital bed scared and confused. I know that she has been in this hospital all night long, and the doctors still don't know what that punk did to her. I know that Romeo needs to pay the price for putting his hands on my wife, so forgive me for not worrying about your precious Desiree. Now if you will excuse me, I have a score to settle." Carl knew Mike was losing control, and he was relieved to see Mike's captain enter the lounge. The captain asked Mike how Rena was doing before escorting him into an empty waiting room. Carl decided to go and check on Desiree while Mike was talking, but before he could leave the floor, Mike's captain came out of the room, leaving Mike visibly upset.

Carl entered the room and closed the door behind him. "What's going on Mike? I just saw your captain and most of the officers leaving."

Mike turned around and kicked the magazine rack in the corner. "My captain wants me to stay put while they go after Romeo. I guess he expects me to sit around here and act like nothing happened"

"It's probably for the best, Mike; besides, Rena needs you here with her."

"Don't tell me what my wife needs," yelled Mike as he turned over a garbage pail. "I don't want the cops to find him and lock him up. I want him myself!"

Mike headed toward the door, but Carl blocked his path. "Don't do this, Mike; if you go out there looking for Romeo, you could end up behind bars yourself."

"Move out of my way," ordered Mike, but Carl stood his ground.

"You can't be involved in this case, Mike; you need to sit this one out. Rena needs you and your place is with her right now."

"I don't need your psychological point of view on where my place is. What I need is for you to stay here and keep an eye on Rena. That punk is getting farther and farther away while everyone is just standing around! Now for the last time, are you going to help me or not?" Carl tried one more time to reason with Mike, but it was to no avail. "Never mind, don't bother," said Mike as he shoved Carl from the door. Carl quickly grabbed Mike's arm. "Let me go," demanded Mike.

"I'm not going to let you do something stupid," insisted Carl. "What if..." But before Carl's next word came to pass, Mike hurled a left hook, catching Carl on the right side of his temple. Carl fell back a few steps but did not go down. "Are you crazy?" he asked, stunned that his best friend actually struck him. "Now I know you're losing it but listen." But it was too late; another blow followed the first one, and this time Carl fell to the floor. He immediately reached up, grabbed Mike's leg, and forced him to the ground. The two men began beating each other while the nurses screamed and banged on the window section of the door for the men to stop fighting. When Rena heard the screams she pulled herself to the side of the bed, where she had a partial view of the fight. She saw Mike stand briefly before Carl knocked him back down, and then she watched helplessly as Carl and Mike fed each other a series of blows. Rena's screams sent Cookie racing from the hospital cafeteria back toward Rena's room. As she approached the room, she saw a crowd of nurses and a few male visitors standing outside the waiting room, banging on the door and yelling for someone to call security. Cookie pushed past the crowd. "Why are you idiots just standing there? Get out of my way!" As the crowd succumbed to Cookie's orders, she flung the door open and entered the room; by now the men were wearing each other out, but neither of them would give up. Cookie reached into her purse, pulled out her container of pepper spray, and sprayed both men until they retreated to separate corners, where they begged for water for their burning eyes. Cookie then placed the cover back on the container and calmly walked out of the waiting room and back into Rena's room to calm her down.

Cookie watched as two nurses helped Rena get back into her bed. As soon as they were able to get her settled, they placed an oxygen mask on her. Rena looked pale and Cookie wondered what actually happened to her. Mike was not talking and Carl appeared to be just as lost as she was, but she was here now and whether Mike liked it or not, she would get to the bottom of what happened.

Cookie was able to help calm Rena down, but there was very little she could do to assure Rena that Mike was okay; in fact, there was no sign of Mike anywhere.

Carl cleaned himself up and went back into Rena's room. "Carl," she cried. "Where is Mike? Why were you two fighting? Are you okay?"

"I'm fine," Carl replied, while trying to ignore the fact that his lip was busted and had started to swell. "I'm sorry you had to see that, Rena. I didn't mean to upset you." Rena began to cry again. "I know Mike didn't mean to attack you. I'm sorry for what he did, Carl, but he's not himself right now." Carl reached over and took Rena's hand. "Don't apologize, Rena. If Lisa was still alive and some man put his hands on her, I would have done the same thing."

Cookie looked over at Carl and asked, "Are you going to tell us what's going on, or should we wait until Rena has a complete breakdown?"

Carl kept his focus on Rena. "Rena, when Mike called me this morning, all he cared about was having me here to protect you."

Cookie gave him a doubtful look. "Mike has an entire

police force behind him, and he called you?"

Carl ignored her. "Rena, you and I both know Mike is out of control right now, and I need to get out there and find him before he does something stupid. Now I can't leave until I know you're okay."

"Please go. I promise I will calm down, just please go and find him, Carl!"

Cookie waited until Carl exited the room, then she turned to Rena. "I forgot to ask Carl something. I'll be right back." Cookie ran down the hall and caught up to Carl. "Rena keeps asking me about Desiree and the baby."

Carl's shoulders dropped as he realized he forgot about checking on Desiree. He reached for his cell phone and called her several times, but each call went straight into voicemail. "Listen, Cookie, I'm going to head over to Desiree's apartment and check on her; will you be able to stay with Rena?"

"Yes, of course I'll stay, but when you get back, we are going to need some answers." Carl rushed through the double doors of the nurse's station and quickly made his way out of the hospital. With Rena lying in a hospital bed, Romeo loose, Mike on a rampage, and Desiree not answering her phone, he found himself right in the middle of all the madness, yet he still had no idea what actually happened.

Carl pulled up to Desiree's building and found it unusually quiet. Looking around for any sign of Mike, he rushed into the building, down the stairs, and through the alley. Carl knocked on Desiree's door several times, but there was no answer. He called out to Desiree, and she finally opened the door. Standing in the doorway with her son in her arms, Carl saw how drained she looked; it was clear that whatever events had taken place the night before had traumatized her. Carl walked inside and Desiree quickly locked the door behind him. "Are you okay?" he asked.

Desiree sank into a chair in the living room and wiped the tears from her eyes. "How is Rena? Does anyone know what Romeo did to her? No one would tell me anything. Gabriel is sick, and I can't get to the hospital. Can you take me to her, Carl? Is she going to be all right?"

Carl pulled an iron-rod chair from the corner and sat down in front of her. "Rena is going to be fine; the paramedics got to her just in time. There is even some speculation that it may have been Romeo who made the call for help."

Desiree lifted her head and in a somber voice she said, "He came after me just like he said he would."

Carl looked around; taking in all there was to the tiny, bare apartment. "Look, Desiree, it's probably not a good idea for you and the baby to stay here alone. Why don't you pack some things and let me take you to your parents' house?"

Desiree shook her head in protest. "We can't go there; my father won't let the baby in the house. Maybe you could take us to the shelter? I know the church has some ties with them. Maybe I can stay there."

Carl was shocked to hear that Desiree felt more welcomed in a shelter than in her own parents' home. "Desiree, that shelter is already full. Is there anyone else you can call?"

Desiree wiped her nose with a tissue and said, "No, there is no one else. He's going to come back; he always does. The cops can't protect us, nobody can. Carl, if you can please drive me around and help me find a cheap motel far away from here, I'll be okay because Romeo won't be able to find me."

Carl now understood Mike's anger; he too wanted to find Romeo and make him pay for putting such fear into Desiree.

"You are not going to any motel, Desiree, especially with the baby. Pack up a few things, and you and the baby can stay at my house." Desiree looked up at him with suspicion, but Carl quickly added, "I'll stay in a hotel nearby and check on the apartment."

"Are you sure, Carl? This is not the safest area to be in."

"You let me worry about that. Just go get your things and we'll get going."

Desiree placed Gabriel into Carl's arms and ran into the bedroom; she was packed and ready to go in five minutes.

"Desiree, before we leave, I need you to tell me a little more about Romeo. I want to know who his friends are, or better yet, where he is likely to go and hide. Does he have family or anyone in the area that he can trust?"

"I really don't know," she replied, while shrugging her shoulders. "He could be anywhere."

Carl stood up and walked toward her. "You spent a lot of time with this man, Desiree, and you know about his life on the streets; now I need you to think. If Romeo were in trouble, what place would he consider to be safe?"

Desiree sensed the irritation in Carl's voice. Just looking at him, she could tell he was tired and he appeared to be stressed; that was so unlike the easy going, confident Carl she had come to know.

Desiree quickly composed her thoughts and told him everything she remembered about Romeo's life on the streets. She told him how Romeo robbed certain stores when he got hungry; where he went when he needed a warm place to sleep and she told him of the few friends she remembered Romeo talking about. Desiree didn't believe Romeo still knew where those friends were. Between Romeo going in and out of jail and his friends doing the same, she was certain his old friends were either dead or locked up; but she told Carl everything she could remember. It was up to him to determine whether or not any of the information was useful.

CHAPTER TEN

The afternoon was cold, and now it started to rain. Romeo regretted making the 911 call; he knew every officer in the county would be looking for him. Romeo needed a safe place to hide, but most of his street connections were either locked up or dead. All alone and with no place else to go, Romeo decided to return to the only home he ever knew. It was the same home where his mother abandoned him, but it was also the same home where his mother held him and sang songs to him, up until the time her new boyfriend came along and changed everything.

The walk to his old neighborhood took him much longer than he anticipated; by now he was tired, cold, and hungry. The old neighborhood was just as dreary and dirty as he remembered it. Romeo moved swiftly down the street, but he was starting to feel lightheaded from hunger. There were a few dogs fighting for the scraps of food left behind by the drug dealers. What he wouldn't give for a morsel of that food to tide him over, but there was no time for that; he needed to hide. Romeo entered the vacant building and began kicking the garbage around until he was able to clear a path to the back of the building. He sat in the area he believed to be his old apartment, but he did not recognize it.

Looking over a pile of wood and metal pipes, he spotted an old futon; he pushed the empty beer bottles, needles, and crack pipes off of it, and then dragged the futon back to his corner to lay down. Right next to him was a large cat feasting on a dead mouse. He ignored their presence, but the stench coming from the self-made bathroom proved to be too much. Romeo closed his eyes and tried to convince himself that his only concern was the smell of urine and not the hunger pains that were now ripping him apart. If only he could fall asleep, he could forget his hunger, or better yet, maybe death would come. Dying had to be better than this, but moments later Romeo did not die; he simply fell asleep.

The sound of sirens blasting woke Romeo, and he jumped up in fear. Even after he realized it was not the police coming for him, Romeo still felt threatened and began to sob. Coming back to his old apartment proved to be a mistake; it brought back painful memories of the mother he missed so much. He saw her a few times, but she was so strung out she did not even recognize him. With all the pain he was experiencing right now, he felt it was time to inflict pain on someone else. There was a grocery store around the corner, and Romeo decided to rob it; only this time instead of demanding money, he would simply walk in, steal a sandwich and a container of milk and make a run for it. Romeo was all set to put his plan into action when the sudden sound of footsteps startled him. Someone had entered the building and was headed his way. Could the cops have found him so quickly? No, it could not be the cops; there would be more of them. This was one person, and the person was walking through the path he had cleared for himself earlier. Romeo stood up and peeked out from behind a partial wall, and was greeted with a fast blow to his right eye. As Romeo's body hit the ground, Carl grabbed him by his collar and began dragging him out of the building. Romeo curled himself up into a ball and began sobbing as he imagined how his life was going to end. "This is it," he thought. "This is how I am going to die. No food, no mother, and no one who would even know I was gone. I am all alone, and this man is going to kill me." Romeo wanted his mother; she never protected him from her boyfriends, but now he wanted to give her one last chance to run in and save him. He wanted his mother to tell this man who was dragging him to his death that she was willing to lay down her own life in exchange for his because that's what mothers did, so he called for her over and over again, but once again she failed to come and save him.

Once they got outside of the building, Carl forced Romeo to his feet and drew him close to his face. Romeo quickly shut his eyes. "Open your eyes!" Carl demanded. As Romeo stood face to face with the man he believed to be his killer, he began to size Carl up. At the very least, he would die fighting for his life. For a brief moment, Romeo was convinced he could actually take the man whom he guessed was around forty years old. Almost as if the old man read his mind, he put one finger in Romeo's face and warned, "If you even think about it, I will take you out right here, and if you ever put your hands on Desiree again, I will hunt you down and show you what a man's beating feels like." Carl then patted Romeo down before dragging him to his car, and forcing him inside.

Romeo was not the hardened street thug Carl had expected to encounter; if he were, he would have fought his way out of that building. It was clear Romeo had very little fight left in him. Carl saw this often enough when he served in the US Marines. There were times you knew a man was just ready to die, and Romeo was that man.

Carl drove carefully, knowing every cop in the area would be searching for Romeo and while he had no problem turning Romeo over to the police, he was more concerned about Mike. Carl was certain, if Mike caught Romeo, he would surely kill him. He knew he had to get Romeo off the street and fast.

Mike got back into his car; the fact that his lip was busted and his nose continued to drip blood did not stop him from roaming through dark alleys and into drug-infested neighborhoods, roughing up anyone he thought could tell him where Romeo was. He was about to try another neighborhood when he spotted a familiar black BMW. Mike studied the motion of the car. Carl was driving at a very careful speed. Mike watched as Carl put on his signal to make a turn, but a red light delayed him. Mike was convinced that Carl either had Romeo in the car with him, or he knew where Romeo was. With his adrenaline pumping, he sped up and pulled right behind Carl's car, and he saw a young male in the passenger seat. As soon as Carl realized Mike was behind him, he pressed down on the accelerator and took off. Mike was able to keep up with him until Carl made an unexpected U-turn and sped off in the opposite direction. Mike slammed on his brakes, causing his vehicle to spin around in a full circle before coming to a stop. With valuable seconds lost, Mike banged on the dashboard, and then he quickly sped up to them.

Carl made one final turn that placed him right in front of the church; he turned to a scared and confused Romeo and said, "Listen, when I say, 'go,' you get out of this car and run up those stairs; you better stay with me, or you'll be dead in five minutes, now go!" Romeo jumped out of the car and ran up the stairs; he took a second to look back to see who was chasing them, but Carl quickly called out, "Keep going! Don't look back!"

Carl pulled the church door open and shoved Romeo inside, leaving him just seconds away from Mike's grip. As the church door slammed shut in Mike's face, he stood there breathing heavily. As angry as he was, he could never show such disrespect to God by going into the church to get Romeo, so he decided to wait.

Forty-five minutes later, the church door opened and Romeo walked out escorted by Pastor Lee and Carl. Mike jumped out of his car and raced up the stairs. Realizing Mike still had not calmed down; Pastor Lee took two steps down the stairs and stood firmly in front of him. "Now you listen to me, Mike, you are out of control, and that makes you a very dangerous man. Now get back in your car and go be with your wife."

Mike glared over Pastor Lee's shoulder. "Turn him loose, Pastor; this is between him and me."

"What are you going to do, Mike? Are you going to shoot this man?"

Mike's response was cold and icy. "With all due respect, Pastor, I have every right to be the judge, jury, and executioner of a man who put his hands on my wife. I also have the authority to remove him from your custody." Pastor Lee got so close to Mike's face he could smell the stench from his sweat. "You got it wrong, son; you are a man of God, and that means you answer to a much higher authority." Mike never took his eyes off of Romeo when he replied, "And what about him Pastor? Doesn't he answer to that same authority?"

"Yes, Mike he does. The only difference is he doesn't know it yet."

Mike slowly went into his jacket and pulled out his badge and held it up to Pastor Lee. "I am ordering you to turn this man over to me; this is police business."

"Mike, I am taking this man down these stairs and into that car. I will drive him to the police station and turn him in myself; now if you believe that gun and badge has more power than the power I am counting on, then go ahead, Detective, take your best shot." Mike stood by breathing heavily and clenching his fist as he watched Pastor Lee and Carl escort a trembling Romeo down the stairs and into the car.

A half hour later, Romeo was being booked; he remained silent throughout the process. He no longer cared about going back to jail or what would happen to him once he got back inside. He had been through it all before anyway. In fact, so much had happened to him in the past twenty-four hours that going back to jail was the only thing that seemed normal to him.

Pastor Lee spoke to Romeo briefly. "Look, son, I don't know whether or not you're guilty of anything, but our church has a legal team. I'm going to ask them to pay you a visit and see to it that you are treated fairly. I'll be back in a day or so, to check on you."

Romeo was then led away in handcuffs and placed into a holding cell. As he sat in his cell, he wondered about the events that brought him back to jail only months after he was released. If that pastor had not stepped in, Romeo knew he would have arrived at the police station severely beaten, if he arrived at all. In his twenty-one years of life, that pastor was the only person who seemed to think his life was worth saving. Romeo wondered if this was the man who fed Desiree all that crazy talk about a God she could not see and a love he could never believe in. He wondered about the man who dragged him out of the building and the crazy detective who wanted to kill him. Encountering these three men was bad enough, but it could not compare to the encounter he had in Desiree's apartment. Romeo shook his head violently; the thought of that light made him shiver and it became perfectly clear to him that something more powerful than he could ever imagine was protecting Desiree and her baby. Romeo already started making plans for what he would do, when he was released. This time instead of trying to go after Desiree again, he would get out and get as far away from her as possible, even if it meant leaving Atlanta.

It was almost midnight when Carl left the station, but he still wanted to check on Desiree. "We're fine, Carl, we found plenty to eat, and your guest room is bigger than my whole apartment!"

"Is Gabriel feeling better?" he asked.

"Yes, he's fine." Desiree did not ask if they caught Romeo, but Carl wanted her to know he was locked up.

"Desiree, I wanted to call and let you know I just left the police station, and they arrested Romeo." Desiree was silent as Carl continued, "I don't want you to go home until we are sure they won't release him. I'll call you in the morning to see if you need anything. In the meantime, I want you to call your mother; she should know what's going on."

"Okay, Carl, I'll call her tomorrow, and thank you again for letting us stay here." Desiree hung up the phone; she knew she would have to let her mother know what had happened, but for now all she wanted to do was enjoy the safety and luxury of Carl's beautiful home.

Carl drove back through Desiree's neighborhood, everything seemed quiet, so he headed for a hotel closer to his own neighborhood and checked in. Room service was available up until one o'clock in the morning. He placed his order before heading up to his room. The events of the night left him mentally and physically drained. Carl unlocked the door, threw his bag and keys on the table, and headed for the shower. Several minutes later, he ate and was settling into bed when his cell phone rang. As soon as he saw the name "Jenna Livingston," he remembered their date.

"Carl, it's Jenna; is everything okay? I thought we had plans for dinner tonight." Jenna's voice was calm, and she appeared to be more concerned about his safety than being stood up. This was a sign of maturity he was pleased to see.

"Jenna, honey, I am so sorry. I can't begin to tell you what my day was like, but you're going to hear about it anyway, so let me fill you in." Jenna could hardly take in all the information Carl was feeding her; she felt incredibly close to him as he confided in her. Jenna listened patiently as Carl told her how hurt he was at having to fight his best friend, how frail Rena looked, and how Cookie maced them. Jenna was glad to hear the bond he had with Mike was now breaking; she did not like Mike at all. "I can't imagine Mike attacking you like that," she said. "You were just trying to keep him from doing something stupid, and that's how he repays you?"

"It's okay, Jenna. I told you I understood why he did it."

"But that doesn't make it right, Carl. You need to stay away from him."

Carl was disappointed in her comments; all he really wanted was a sympathetic ear, not more conflict. "Jenna, I'm going to the hospital in the morning to see Rena. Would you like to come?"

Jenna ignored his offer. "Well, did they catch this Romeo guy? I can't believe Desiree got Rena into all this mess!"

"It's not Desiree's fault," Carl replied.

Jenna's temper began to flare; she hated when Carl defended her. "Are you telling me Desiree's thug boyfriend beats her up, she drags Rena into it, Rena ends up in the hospital, and none of this is Desiree's fault?" Jenna's voice was cold and harsh, and Carl was beginning to feel more drained than before.

"Jenna, I thought you would want to know what happened to your friend and why I didn't show up for our date tonight. I'm sorry if all of this upset you. Listen, I need to get some sleep; can I call you in the morning?"

"Wait, Carl, I'm the one who should apologize. All this has taken me by surprise; I didn't mean to sound so cold. Listen, I made some soup earlier; why don't I bring some over? It sounds like you could use something hot that goes down easy."

"Thanks, Jenna, but what I need now is some sleep; besides, I just had a very late dinner."

"Carl, I'm worried about you, and I need to see that you're okay."

Carl managed to smile; this was the reaction he wanted from her earlier. He needed a sympathetic ear.

"I'm okay, Jenna, but that was nice to hear. Why don't I pick you up in the morning? We can have breakfast before we go see Rena."

"Carl, you only live thirty minutes away; what's wrong with me dropping something by for you?"

"Well, first of all, Jenna, I don't want you driving by yourself this time of night, and besides that, I'm not home, I'm staying in a hotel for a few days. Desiree was terrified when I stopped in to check on her; she was convinced Romeo was coming back for her, so I let her and the baby stay in my house for a few days. Now what about breakfast tomorrow? We could get an early start, grab a quick bite and then go see Rena. I think it would do her some good to have her friends there. She could really use the support."

Jenna was silent for several minutes; she could not

believe Carl gave up his home to Desiree. She tried to compose her anger before she spoke. "Let me get this straight; you moved into a hotel and gave your home to Desiree and that baby? Is there something you're not telling me about your relationship with Desiree?"

"No, Jenna," he replied. "I know it seems a bit drastic, but I couldn't just leave them there."

"Carl, can I ask you something?"

"Of course," he replied.

"Are you sleeping with Desiree?"

Carl was becoming more and more disappointed in Jenna, but he tried to imagine how this must look to her. "No, Jenna, I am not sleeping with Desiree."

"Well, then let me ask you another question. Are you at all attracted to me?"

"I think you know the answer to that, Jenna; why are you playing games with me?"

"Then why won't you let me come over, and how come you let me go home alone after our date last week? You knew I wanted to be with you that night."

Carl was a little thrown off by Jenna's boldness, but his reply was casual, "Jenna, as far as me letting you go home alone that night, all I can say is when we first met, I believed I would have to work very hard to ever get that close to you. I can see now, you were simply lowering your standards. It seems like I am getting to know the real Jenna now."

"Don't you dare judge me," she yelled.

"I am not judging you, Jenna; look, can we talk about this in the morning?"

"No," she yelled. "You started this, so let's finish it! You're not the man you pretend to be. You may not be sleeping with Desiree, but you want to. No man does those things for a woman and expects nothing in return. And what about Cookie? We still have not talked about your night with her! I guess you expected me to forget about that didn't you?"

Carl had heard enough; it was becoming clear to him that Jenna was unstable. As her voice continued to creep through his phone, Carl pressed the end-call button and felt immediate relief. He got up and went to the mini fridge and took out a bottle of water, but before he could take a sip, his cell phone rang again. Carl knew it was Jenna calling him back so he ignored the call and climbed back into bed. Clearly Jenna was not the woman for him; that revelation was confirmed when he realized that after everything he told her about Rena, she never once asked if her friend was okay.

CHAPTER ELEVEN

When Carl woke; he was still a little sore but feeling much better. Looking over at the alarm clock, he was relieved to know he woke early enough to have his coffee and regroup before heading to the university. He turned on the lamp and the television, then ordered his breakfast.

Carl finally felt like he was able to relax. After his miserable weekend, he looked forward to spending the day with his students; most of them were smart, but there were a handful of extremely bright students whom he enjoyed teaching the most. Carl could not think of a better place he would rather be.

The morning went by quickly as a handful of his students were engaged in a debate about economic growth. This was the kind of stimulation Carl loved. Preparing young men and women to take on the world was what he lived for, and there was no doubt that some of these students were ready. Carl allowed the debate to continue on for a few minutes more, and then he reluctantly ended class.

Later that afternoon Carl headed for his favorite cafe off campus. When he arrived, the owner, Mr. Carmine, quickly pulled him aside. "Professor Dupree, I wasn't sure you were coming in today."

"What happened, Carmine, did you give away my table?"

said Carl with a laugh, but Mr. Carmine's demeanor remained serious as he wiped his hands on his apron.

"There is a detective here, and he asked if he could sit and wait for you. He's been here awhile. I didn't know what to do, so I told him he could wait." Carl glanced over, and from a distance he could see the man at his table was Mike. "It's okay, Carmine. He's a friend of mine, but thanks for the heads up." Mr. Carmine breathed a sigh of relief. Carl was one of his favorite customers, and he admired the way he mentored his students. It was good to know the detective was here out of friendship and nothing more. Carl walked toward the back of the café, making his way through the narrow rows of tables. Mike was sitting with his back toward the door. As Carl approached the table, Mike put down his cup of coffee and folded his newspaper, letting Carl know he was aware of his presence.

"Any reason you're sitting with your back to the door?" Carl asked.

Mike's voice was dry but not harsh.

"Well, I thought I would give you a free shot at me, if you wanted one."

"Like I would really need to sneak up on you," said Carl as he laughed, pulled out a chair, and sat down.

Mike looked over at Carl. "Listen, man, about the other night..."

"Stop," said Carl, holding his hand up. "You don't need to say it."

"Yes, I do," insisted Mike. "Just hear me out. The night all of this went down, Rena and I argued, and I stormed out of the house. Things between us have been so tense, she's angry all the time and to tell you the truth, I'd rather be in the streets dodging bullets than home with her. Anyway, I made a few stops, before heading to the station. I usually call her, but that day I avoided talking to her; in fact, I avoided going home for dinner. When I finally did get home, it was a little after nine and she was gone. I knew she was mad, but I didn't think it was that serious; anyway, I kept calling her, but she didn't answer. I drove back to the station and that's when I heard the call come in over the radio. I knew it was Desiree's place, and I realized Rena must have gone there to help her." Mike's voice was strained, and his eyes told the story of a sleep-deprived man. The waiter returned to the table and refilled Mike's coffee cup, then placed a fresh cup of coffee in front of Carl. "Anyway, like I was saying, after several attempts to reach her, I get some police officer answering my wife's phone; he tells me an incident just occurred and that I needed to get to Desiree's apartment. By the time I arrived, they had already taken Rena to the hospital, so I raced over there but no one could tell me what happened to her. That's when I lost it. I kept thinking how scared she must have been and how I was not there to protect her." Mike paused and took a few sips of his coffee. "You know, that was the longest hour of my life. When the doctor finally came out, all he said was, 'She's stable for now, but there are signs of trauma; she could have fallen or have been knocked to the ground, we don't know yet.' "I was ready to kill Romeo with my bare hands."

"So what actually happened?" Carl asked. "Did Romeo attack Rena thinking she was Desiree?"

"I still don't know," replied Mike. Rena blacked out and can't remember much. James Marshall went to the jail to meet with Romeo, and he seems to think Romeo is telling the truth when he said he never saw or touched Rena."

"And you don't believe him?" asked Carl.

"I don't know what to believe. Romeo has a long criminal record that includes domestic violence, breaking and entering, and theft; you can't exactly take him at face value. The bottom line is he went to that apartment planning to harm Desiree; something scared him off, and he climbed back out of the window and started to run away. That's when he claims to have seen Rena laying on the living room floor. He thought it was Desiree and called the police. Turns out he may have saved my wife's life."

Carl watched as Mike finally started to show signs of remorse for going after Romeo. Mike shook his head and in a very somber voice stated, "If I had caught Romeo that night..."

"But you didn't catch him," said Carl. "And I have the burn marks on the soles of my shoes to prove it." Carl tried to lighten the mood, but Mike remained serious.

"I didn't catch him because some lunatic had my back and kept me from losing everything. Look, Carl, you know I never would have swung at you like that. I can't believe I lost control like that. I'm sorry, man."

"I know," replied Carl. I really should have used better restraint too. I knew you weren't yourself that night." Carl was ready to change the subject; he knew Mike was sorry, and he also felt bad about fighting his friend. "Looks like you've been hitting the gym lately; those blows were coming quickly," said Carl.

"I have to," replied Mike. "I'm thirty-seven, but I feel like an old man chasing these street kids."
The waiter returned with Carl's meal and set it in front of him. "How is Rena doing? I wanted to get over to the hospital this morning to see her, but I didn't make it. I'll probably go this evening."

"She's better; in fact, they released her this morning."

"I'm glad to hear that," replied Carl as he inspected

his sandwich.

Mike pushed his seat back and laughed as he looked over at Carl. "You know, the funny thing is, I talked you into moving to Atlanta so Rena and I could help you rebuild your life, but it looks like we were the ones who needed you more."

Mike extended his hand, and Carl reached over and shook it. "You know, moving here has actually been good for me. I love teaching at the university. I have a new church family, and when I add in you, Rena, and all of her crazy friends, life here is never dull."

Mike laughed. "Speaking of Rena's crazy friends, I hear you and Jenna have been testing the waters."

"No, that ship sank already," said Carl. "Our first date was a real disaster, but we worked it out, and our second date was good, but Jenna's not the one; but it was nice knowing I could respond to another woman like that again. After Lisa died, I didn't think it was possible."

"Well, you know Lisa was a little nutty too," said Mike, and he laughed.

Carl threw his napkin at Mike. "See, that's why you got that first, beat down."

Mike kept laughing "I am telling you, Carl, you'd be better off anchoring yourself to the bottom of the sea than trying to figure Jenna out; she's a real head case."

"What's wrong with her?" Carl asked.

"Everything is wrong with Jenna. You would need a team of therapists for that crazy woman. Jenna can be nice and civil to you one minute, then in the blink of an eye, she can unleash her fury; and you never see it coming. When Jenna gets mad, no one is safe, not even Jay."

"Okay, so Jenna flips out on people, you still haven't told me what it is that makes her so angry." Carl replied.

"Jenna is wounded." said Mike. She had some boyfriend awhile back. I think his name was Maurice. They dated for ten years, and he broke up with her the night before his wedding. It tore her up badly."

"So that's where all this anger comes from?" asked Carl.

"It's hard to believe a person can allow one bad relationship to mess them up for life, but I see this kind of behavior on the street and in the jails every day. The problem is, everyone else can see how angry Jenna is, except Jenna. I think Jay even knows her sister is a little crazy, but she's lived with her so long, she's just immune to it."

"Well it still seems like something more must have happened for Jenna to be that angry." said Carl.

"Yeah, there's more, I think Jenna is still mad about her parent's divorce. Seems like the mother divorced their father, ran off with some man and sent Jenna and Jay to live with their grandmother. Jenna ended up having to take care of Jay; their grandmother is up in age and she doesn't have much money so Jenna became the real bread winner for the three of them. I guess she's under a lot of pressure."

"I guess I can understand her frustration." replied Carl.

Mike realized his friend had already fallen for Jenna, and he did not want to witness that train wreck, so he changed the subject. "The house looks good, and I see you added the extra bedroom to the basement. I may need to crash there soon, so don't take in any tenants."

Carl gave Mike a brief stare. "I guess that means things with you and Rena are really sour? Are you two going to be okay?"

"I don't know," replied Mike. "Do you know the other night we argued over who would put the key in the door?"

"Are you serious?" asked Carl.

"I'm telling you, things between us are that bad. I don't know why Rena resents me, but it's draining the life out of me."

"Mike, are you telling me you're living in the same house with your wife, and you have no idea what's bothering her?"

Mike looked over at Carl. "Yeah, pretty much the way you didn't know what was bothering Jenna."

"I've known Jenna two weeks; you have been married to Rena for years."

Mike paused for several minutes, and then he replied, "Well, it's never about one thing with Rena, but to start, you know she wants a baby. We have been trying for nearly two years and I think she's getting scared. Rena feels like it's never going to happen. When she isn't crying over not being pregnant, she's sharing her frustration about me not letting her start her own catering business."

"Well, what's wrong with her starting a catering business? Rena is a very good cook and it would keep her busy and bring in some extra money."

"Rena doesn't want to start a business." Mike replied. "All she wants is something else to hold over my head. It's like she's building a case against me."

Carl looked puzzled. "Okay, Mike, you lost me."

"Think about it Carl, Rena is asking me for fifteen hundred dollars to start a catering business; when you factor in advertising, supplies and the additional help she is going to need to get this business going, do you really think fifteen hundred dollars is enough?"

"Okay, you may have a point there Mike, but if it makes her happy to try, then why not support her? It's not like you can't afford it. Your home is already paid off, so what's the real issue here?"

"The real issue is I have an angry wife and I don't know what to do about it."

Carl pushed his plate to the side and leaned toward Mike. "Mike, you make a living pulling information out of people who don't want to talk to you. Are you sure you don't know what's bothering Rena, or do you not want to know?"

Carl waited for Mike to reply and when he didn't Carl made one final comment. "Listen Mike, everyone knows marriage is not always easy, but Rena is a good woman and she is certainly worth fighting for. Don't make the mistake of thinking she will always be around."

Mike sipped the last of his coffee and held his head down; there he was complaining about his wife, knowing Carl would probably give anything to have Lisa back. Mike decided he did not want to talk about his marriage anymore; he looked up at Carl, but his only response to him was, "I hear you."

"So are you going to stay and eat?" asked Carl.

"No, I have to get back. Rena is home with her mom, and I promised them I would be home for lunch." Mike stood up and started to button his jacket. "Oh, before I forget, do you know what Pastor Lee is asking me to do?" Before Carl could answer, Mike sat down again and leaned toward him. "James Marshall looked into Romeo's case, and the courts are coming down hard on him; he'll be in jail for a long time."

"And that's exactly where he belongs," answered Carl.

"Agreed," said Mike. "But Pastor Lee wants me to be Romeo's mentor. I told him as grateful as I am for Romeo making that phone call, I am not playing big brother to that thug."

Carl looked at him and casually asked, "Why not?"

Mike gave Carl a questionable stare. "You don't think Pastor Lee has lost his mind asking me to mentor Romeo?"

"No," replied Carl. "I think he's doing exactly what he said he would do." Carl sat up sternly, and with a grin on his face he imitated Pastor Lee. "It is my mission to create a lost-and-found program in this church. What good is it for all the people in church to be saved and our brothers and sisters outside these doors to be lost?"

Mike laughed. "Okay, point taken, but I'm still not doing it. Romeo had no business going after Desiree. She did all of the right things this time; we locked him up and he still came out and did the same thing. I am so tired of this cat and mouse game. Romeo is a bully and a thug and I won't waste my time with him."

"Look Mike, I don't like Romeo either, but did you really stop to think about the events of that night? If Romeo had not gone to Desiree's apartment that night, Rena may have laid on that floor a lot longer and the paramedics said they arrived with only minutes to save her. Like it or not Mike, Romeo could have saved Rena's life."

"Well, I'm not singing praises for Romeo just yet. I deal in facts and the fact is, Romeo was operating under a dark influence that night, and that dark influence led him to believe that harming Desiree was okay. I just wish I knew what scared him away. I spoke to James Marshall and he said Romeo refuses to tell anyone what caused him to run out of Desiree's apartment that night; but whatever it was terrified him."

Mike stood up and started to button his jacket. "Listen, I have to go, but before I forget, Rena wants you and Cookie to come over for dinner sometime this week; she's worried about everyone, and she won't rest until she sees everyone is okay."

"Tell Rena I would love to come to dinner as long as Cookie is kept on a tight leash. I still can't believe she walks around with pepper spray, and clearly she is not afraid to use it." said Carl.

Mike was quiet for several minutes; then he looked down at his friend and replied, "I'm just glad Cookie was there." Mike positioned himself to give Carl a hug. Carl quickly stood up, hugged Mike, and said, "Go on, man, get out of here and go check on your wife."

"Yeah, I'm going," replied Mike, then he grabbed half of Carl's sandwich and left.

CHAPTER TWELVE

Saturday morning arrived. The week had gone by way too fast and now it was time for Desiree and Gabriel to return home. Desiree woke to find Gabriel staring up at her. She pulled her son close to her and laughed at his innocence. Desiree was so thankful for her son; he bought so much joy into her life.

Desiree finished cleaning up the guest room and dressed Gabriel. "Come on baby, Aunt Rena will be here soon to take us home." In spite of having to leave today, Desiree was very excited about their trip downtown to buy Gabriel's new stroller. After months of saving, she finally had enough money to purchase a good stroller for her son; she locked up Carl's house and went outside to wait for Rena.

The warm air felt good and the colorful plants outside of Carl's house made Desiree feel like she was in a beautiful garden. Desiree had never been in such a beautiful home before. As she stood outside the doorway of his home, she noticed a plaque Carl had inscribed on a block of stone that sat outside his doorway. Desiree read it over and over again; it said, "A kind man will follow his heart; but a wise man will follow God."

Desiree laughed as she watched Gabriel try to catch a butterfly in his little hands; then she looked up to God and said, "I guess I was wrong God; I told you I did not believe there were any men in this world that would not hurt me or try to take advantage of me; but when Gabriel and I were in trouble, you sent us Carl. Being wrong never felt this good before! Thank you God!"

A few minutes later, Rena pulled up into Carl's driveway. "So how did you like living in the mansion?" Rena asked.

"One day, I'm going to own a home just like this," replied Desiree.

Gabriel began smiling at the sight of Rena, and then engaged her in a game of peek-a-boo.

"He's such a happy baby. I can't wait until Mike and I have one of our own." Jay was seated in the passenger side of Rena's truck, and as soon as she heard Rena's comment about wanting a baby, she opened the door and shouted, "Can you two stop all this talk about babies and get in the car!"

Desiree's eyes shifted toward Jay. "Hi, Jay. I didn't know you were coming with us."

"I'm going downtown too. I need to find shoes for my wedding. Jenna was supposed to take me, but thanks to your friend Carl, she's too depressed to do anything. Now come on and put the baby in the car. I have a lot of shopping to do."

"Sure, Jay, it's all about you," replied Desiree.

It only took them a few minutes to reach the shopping center. "I see a parking space up front," said Desiree, but as soon as Rena tried to move into it, another car managed to beat her to the spot.

"Why don't you just let me out here." complained Jay. "We've been circling this block for ten minutes now."

"You're going to wait with the rest of us," replied

Rena. "Besides, we need to get the baby's stroller first, so we can all walk around together."

"Fine," replied Jay. "Let me know when you guys find a spot; I'm taking a quick nap."

A few minutes later, Rena found a parking space right in front of the baby store. "Desiree, why don't you run in and get the stroller? Jay and I will wait here with the baby."

"Sounds good to me," said Desiree as she exited the car. "Mommy will be right back with your new stroller, honey." Desiree entered the store and quickly made her way to the baby section; she was so excited about purchasing the new stroller until she actually saw them. The advertisement boasted a selection of colorful strollers with toys attached to them, but Desiree quickly discovered those strollers did not exist. There were only two strollers in her price range; one was black with red-and-white checkers, and the other was gray with black stitching around the edges. Desiree looked the gray stroller over; she was disappointed, but the stroller was strong and sturdy, so she pushed it up to the cashier. "How will you be paying for this?"

"Cash," replied Desiree.

The cashier rang up the sale. "That will be $189."

Desiree quickly handed her the store flyer. "I have your flyer that says this stroller is on sale until tomorrow for $140."

The cashier was unmoved and coldly replied, "Oh, that was a misprint. If you want the stroller, it will be $189."

Desiree's heart sank; she budgeted $140 for the stroller and not a penny more. The customers waiting in line began to get impatient, and the cashier asked Desiree to move aside until she made up her mind. Placing the money back in her purse, she held back her tears of frustration and left the store.

"What happened to the stroller?" asked Jay.

"There was some misprint, and the price went up."

"Oh well, I guess we can go get my shoes now. Come on, Rena, let's go."

Rena was on the phone with Mike and did not realize Desiree was in the truck until Gabriel began to cry.

"What's the matter with him?" asked Jay.

Rena turned her attention to Gabriel and asked, "What's the matter with Aunt Rena's baby?"

Desiree looked around for Gabriel's cup. "I forgot his cup; he's hot and probably wants his juice."

"Must he cry that loudly?" complained Jay.

Desiree struggled to find his cup but gave up after a few minutes. "I'll just run in the store and get him another cup. I'm sorry, guys; I will only be a minute."

As she got out of the truck and closed the door, she could hear Jay complaining about being delayed and having to listen to a crying baby. Fortunately, the store was fairly empty, and she was able to purchase the cup quickly. As she was about to exit the store, another stroller caught her attention; she was certain that stroller had not been there before. Admiring it from afar, Desire could already tell this stroller was even more expensive than the one she had intended to buy, but it was so beautiful that she couldn't stop staring at it. A sales clerk carrying a large red tag under her arm walked over to the stroller and stapled the red tag over the regular price. Desiree felt certain, even with a sale tag attached to it, the stroller would still be out of her price range but curiosity got the best of her. She walked over to the stroller, turned the tag over, and gasped. The bright red tag read, "Clearance price seventy dollars."

Desiree barely heard the sales clerk standing next to her. "It's beautiful, isn't it? Some lady came in here months ago and left a deposit on it and never came back. My manager told me to put it out last week, but I couldn't find it. Then early this morning, I went downstairs to take inventory and there it was. I was on my way to lunch when something reminded me to put the stroller out."

Desiree could not focus on the saleswoman; she was too busy running her hands across the plush cushion padding that was decorated with blue, yellow, and green teddy bears. The stroller had a canopy, a cup holder, and a serving tray, and the bottom part of the stroller held a removable basket. Desiree was thrilled; finally she could carry her groceries home while pushing her son in a nice sturdy stroller. "Well, I guess this was meant for me," she said as she pushed the stroller up to the cashier and made the purchase.

Desiree headed outside and back to Rena's truck; she was beaming and not even Jay's complaints bothered her. Jay stuck her head out of the window and yelled to Desiree, "You heard this baby crying. I told you I had a lot of shopping to do Desiree, what took you so long?"

Desiree loaded the stroller into the back of Rena's truck and slipped into the back seat with her son. "Sorry, Jay, but God had something put away for me."

Rena turned around and smiled at her. "He sure does take good care of you, Desiree." With tears in her eyes, Desiree poured juice into her son's cup, then she leaned back and closed her eyes. All she wanted was a quiet moment to thank God for the stroller.

Jay turned to Desiree and with a confused expression, she asked, "Who? Who takes care of you? Are you two going to start talking about that God mess again?"

"It's not mess," replied Rena. "And we never stop talking about Him; you must know that by now."

"Oh, please! Can we just go? I have a wedding to get

ready for, and I don't want to be trapped in this car with that baby screaming and the two of you preaching that nonsense again!"

CHAPTER THIRTEEN

Jenna was sitting in her lounge chair thinking about the upcoming buyer's showcase. Some of the top buyers in the industry would soon fill the busy streets of New York City, and Jenna desperately wanted Carl to attend the event with her. Carl would be the perfect companion for this high-profile affair, but he would not return any of her phone calls. Jenna knew there was one way she could get Carl's attention, and she would use Desiree to do it. One act of kindness toward Desiree would certainly land her back in Carl's arms again. Jenna took a few minutes to develop her plan; when she was ready to put it into action, she picked up her cell phone and called Carl. After five rings the call went into voicemail. "Carl, this is Jenna. I need your help. I'm hoping to get Desiree's evening bags into a showcase in New York next month. The buyers are looking for new designers and...well, please call me back. I don't have Desiree's number and I really don't want to bother Rena while she's recovering."

Jenna hung up the phone and began biting her lip. Making the call to Carl was easy, even though she really didn't need Desiree's phone number. Jenna knew she could get Desiree's bags into the showcase and if everything went according to plan, Carl would come to the showcase to see what she was able to do for Desiree, and that meant she had to pull out all the stops to impress him. Jenna moved forward with the second part of her plan and called Jay.

"Hey, Jen, what's up?"

"Jay, can you come over? I need a huge favor."

"No, I can't. I'm looking at bridal catalogues. I still haven't found my dress, my shoes, or anything else."

"Well, that's why I'm calling, Jay. I'm going to New York next month to cover a showcase; the person giving the event is a friend of mine. I'm going to ask him to give Desiree a booth in the show, but Wilfred does not allow new designers to showcase their own material, which means Desiree will need a host."

"Sounds like a personal problem to me," replied Jay as she continued to flip through the magazine.

Jenna sighed; this was so typical of her sister. "Jay, can I please finish my point? I'll pay for all of your expenses while we are in New York if you agree to work Desiree's booth."

"New York?" asked Jay, suddenly interested.

"Yes," replied Jenna. "All you have to do is host the booth during the private showing; after that you can move around the showroom and see some of the work from real designers."

"Seriously, Jenna, I can go with you? I heard about this showcase at work. I heard Miss Millie is planning to attend this event herself! I read where she is interested in a new line of bridal gowns for her stores in London!" Jenna was impressed with her sister's knowledge of the industry. "Do you think you can introduce me to Miss Millie Montgomery, Jenna?"

"First of all, Jay, I don't know the lady, and from what I hear she is not very friendly."

"Well, at least I can shop for my dress while I'm there."

"You cannot afford those dresses, Jay; besides, these showcases are for buyers, and the designers don't sell to individuals."

"Well, what if I buy one of the sample dresses?" asked Jay.

"The sample dresses will start out at ten thousand dollars, and those will be the rejects," said Jenna.

Jay was silent for a minute, then asked, "Well, can you buy my dress for me? Nana wants to pay for it, but she can't afford the kind of dress I want."

At first Jenna did not respond; in addition to her being jealous of her younger sister getting married, she did not approve of Jay marrying Luther. Luther worked as a security guard, and Jenna was convinced this marriage would render Jay hopelessly poor. "I will commit to seven thousand dollars and not a penny more." Jay jumped up from her couch with excitement. "Thanks, Jenna! Now when do we leave?"

"In three weeks," replied Jenna. "Can you get time off from work?"

"That shouldn't be a problem," said Jay. "I'm so excited. I can't wait to go! I'm going to call my boss now and request the time off; bye Jenna." Jay hung up and Jenna sighed as she prepared to make her next phone call.

Desiree's phone rang three times before her voicemail message came on. "Hi Desiree, this is Jenna. If you can make it to New York next month, I can get your bags into a showcase; call me back and I will give you the details."

No sooner than Jenna hung up, Desiree called back and informed Jenna that Rena was also on the line. Jenna rolled her eyes as she listened to the excitement in their voices. With only three weeks left until the show, Jenna reminded them both, that her reputation was on the line and to make sure the bags and the booth were up to Wilfred's standards, then she hung up. Carl was the only thing that mattered to her, and if helping Desiree was the only way to get back into Carl's life, then she was happy to do it.

The next phone call she made was to Wilfred; he agreed to give Desiree a booth in the Blue Room. At first, Wilfred tried to offer Jenna a discounted price, of fifteen hundred dollars; but after Jenna reminded him that she had the ability to help or hurt his showcase; Wilfred agreed to give Desiree a free booth. Having Jenna on his side was more important than collecting the three thousand dollars, from Desiree.

Jenna spent the next three weeks shopping for dresses, perfume and lingerie; she mapped out some of the restaurants and exhibits she knew Carl would like. This time she was certain that Carl would take her back and she wanted to be ready for him.

CHAPTER FOURTEEN

The drive from Atlanta to New York was a long one. Jenna and Jay arrived to their hotel at three o'clock in the morning and went right to sleep.

The next morning, Jenna woke with the feeling of butterflies in her stomach. There was so much riding on this day. Carl had finally returned her call, but only long enough to give her Desiree's phone number. When she asked him about coming to New York, he simply said he would think about it. That was not the response she was hoping for, but at least he was talking to her again. Jenna opened the sliding door that lead to the balcony and sat down to have her coffee. Their hotel suite had a magnificent view of midtown Manhattan. As she sat watching the busy streets of New York City, she could only imagine how impressed Carl would be when he saw what she was able to do for Desiree. Feeling confident her plan had worked, she placed her coffee cup on the patio table and went inside to wake her sister. "Wake up, Jay; today is the big day, and we have a lot of work to do."

Jay bounced up so quickly it made Jenna laugh. "I'm surprised you were able to sleep, as excited as you were last night." Jay did not respond; instead, she grabbed her bags and headed for the bathroom. Twenty minutes later, the two sisters were dressed and on their way to

Fifth Avenue.

There was so much traffic in New York City; Jenna could not believe it was taking so long to get to their destination. "Jay, hand me my phone please. I need to call Rena and make sure they get Desiree here on time."

As soon as Rena saw it was Jenna calling, she answered the phone with a cheerful greeting. "Hi, Jenna."

"Hi, Rena. I'm just calling to check in; where are you?"

"We're still driving, but we should be there in less than an hour."

Jenna took a deep breath before asking her next question. "So who else is with you and Desiree?"

"Just her mom and the baby; Desiree had so much stuff there was no way we could fit anyone else in the truck."

"You mean it's just the four of you?"

"Yes," replied Rena. "But don't worry; she is well prepared. Katherine and Evelyn Johnson stayed up late last night putting the finishing touches on her evening bags, and they are beautiful."

Jenna hung up the phone and her heart sank; she didn't care about Desiree's bags. All she really cared about was impressing Carl, and now after all of her hard work, Carl did not even care enough to show up? Jenna quickly became furious. Did Carl really think he could accept her help, and then simply dismiss her again? Did he realize everything she did for Desiree could easily be undone in a matter of minutes? At that moment, Jenna decided to pull the plug on Desiree's showcase. "Jay, stop daydreaming and look for the address like I told you to," snapped Jenna.

"All right, Jenna, you don't have to bite my head off. And just for the record, you never asked me to look for any address."

"Please shut up, Jay. I'm stuck fighting this traffic, and we're already running late."

"Well, it's not my fault," pleaded Jay. "My goodness, Jenna, what bug crawled up your butt now?"

"Hand me my cell phone, Jay. I need to make a call." When Jay was slow to respond, Jenna pulled the car over and snatched Jay's phone from her.

Jay was furious; she quickly found her sister's cell phone and shoved it at her. "Here, use your own phone."

Jenna dialed and waited nervously for Wilfred to answer. "This is Wilfred, darling, and you should feel honored that I answered your call."

"Wilfred, this is Jenna."

"Darling! My sweet Jenna, how are you?"

"Wilfred, I need another favor."

"Darling, I have already given your friend the best location possible; she is all set to showcase from the Blue Room, I am sorry darling, I can do no more!" Wilfred was as dramatic as they came and Jenna was sick of his phony English accent.

"Wilfred, my friend can't make it to the showcase today, and she sent another designer to take her place. I'm afraid I can no longer vouch for the quality of the evening bags that will be displayed. Can you tuck this designer somewhere in the back with the other entry-level designers?"

"There are no other entry-level designers in this showcase," he yelled. "How could you do this to me, Jenna? Do you know the clientele I have coming to my showcase? I received word that Miss Millie herself is interested in seeing my showcase and I have designers who are paying me thousands of dollars for a booth, and you expect me to set them up next to a Popsicle designer! Are you trying to destroy me Jenna?"

Jenna knew Wilfred was being way too dramatic, but he was extremely sensitive about his shows. "Please, Wilfred, just move her booth for me. I can't risk anyone seeing the bags, and I certainly don't want anyone to write up a review on this designer."

Wilfred realized he was wasting valuable time battering Jenna when he should be figuring out a way to save his show from her tacky designer friend. With his reputation now on the line, Wilfred quickly composed a new plan. "Okay, here's what we'll do, there's a booth in the Brown section of the loft. The designers go there to practice their layouts; I let them use that location when they need privacy. I'll have your friend set up in that area."

"Thank you, Wilfred. I really appreciate it, and I am really sorry about all of this."

"Save your apology Jenna. Just know from this moment on, you and I are through, as friends and business associates. This stunt is by far the most unprofessional thing you have ever done." Wilfred slammed the phone down in Jenna's ear, and Jenna fought hard to control her temper. Normally, she would never tolerate abuse from anyone, but she needed Wilfred's cooperation, so she let it go.

"Is everything okay?" asked Jay.

"Please shut up, Jay, and let me think. Better yet, don't say another word to me until we get to the showroom." Jay was hurt, and she was growing tired of Jenna's abuse. As excited as she was about coming to New York, she now wished she had stayed home. The chances of her meeting Miss Millie were looking slim, and she wondered if she would even be allowed to try on the bridal gowns; she missed Luther, New York City was way too busy for her comfort, and now she found herself trapped in a car with her emotionally unstable sister.

A half hour later, they arrived to their location. "Come on, Jay. I only have a few minutes before my first interview. Help me get the things out of the trunk."

As they began unloading Jenna's recording devices and expensive cameras from the trunk, Jay looked around the parking lot in amazement. "Wow, Jenna, look at all the stuff those people are unpacking. I guess they plan to really set their booths up nicely." Jenna turned around to see a few designers she recognized; apparently, they were given preferential treatment and allowed to set up their booths early. They watched as the designers bought in stage lights, crystal tables, and silk paintings to use as props for their displays. "I hope Desiree has stuff like that for her booth," said Jay.

"Don't be ridiculous, Jay. Where on earth would Desiree get such expensive props?"

Jay's response was casual as she fished items out of the trunk. "From Carl. He borrowed some things from the university's drama department. Desiree has lights and rotating stands, and some of his students sent their artwork for her to use as a backdrop. Rena said it's pretty nice stuff."

Jenna rolled her eyes and was about to start walking when her sister's next comment hit her like a ton of bricks. "Rena also said she was glad Carl came along to show them how to use all of the props."

Jenna froze. "What do you mean, Carl came along? Rena said it was just her, Desiree, and her mom."

"No, the baby's here too; that's why Carl and Mike had to take another car. They couldn't fit everything in Rena's truck, so Mike drove his truck with all the heavy stuff."

Jenna was now in a state of panic. "Are you sure Jay? Because I spoke to Rena, and she didn't mention any of that to me."

Jay began shaking the dust out of her magazine as she filled her sister in on the details. "While you were on the phone with Wilfred, Carl tried to call you, and when you didn't pick up, he called me. He wanted to see you before your interview; he said something about getting some coffee or lunch after you were done."

"Jay! How could you be so stupid? Why didn't you say something to me sooner?"

Jay ignored the insult and calmly replied, "Well, you told me not to say another word to you until we got here, so I didn't." Jenna stood in disbelief at what Jay had done. There was no doubt in her mind that Jay was being vindictive by not giving her Carl's message. Jenna grabbed her travel bag from the trunk, then slammed the trunk shut with no concern for Jay, who was still pulling her items out of the trunk. "You almost slammed the trunk down on me!" Jay cried. Jenna walked out of the parking lot, pulling her thousand-dollar travel bag behind her while quietly sorting out the best plan of revenge for Jay. The one thing Jay wanted more than anything was to be married in a designer gown, and that could not happen without her help, so Jenna made the decision not to purchase Jay's wedding dress. Satisfied with the level of punishment she would inflict on Jay, she breathed a sigh of relief. That would teach Jay not to cross her again.

As they walked up Fifth Avenue, Jay could hardly keep up with her sister, whose energy seemed to be fueled by anger. When they finally arrived at the address, Jay looked up at the old building with disappointment. "Is this it? I thought it would look better than this."

"The outside of the building doesn't matter Jay; there are designers in this building with real talent. What and how they display is really all that counts," replied Jenna.

"Still, I can't believe Miss Millie Montgomery would travel all the way from London to come to a dump like this," said Jay. Jenna led her sister up a long staircase and through the doors, where a crowd of designers waited to register. Jay was tickled by the attention her sister received once the designers realized Jenna was there to cover the showcase. Jay followed Jenna to the front of the line, where they were greeted by a young man dressed in a lime-green jumpsuit who introduced himself as Tiny. Tiny was Wilfred's assistant; he handed Jenna a program guide, two brown tickets, and a map with the locations of the top designers clearly marked. Tiny then led them into one of the most spectacular showrooms Jenna had ever seen; he gave Jenna a few instructions, before excusing himself.

"Jay, my 8:15 interview is here, so you will have to entertain yourself for a while."

"What am I supposed to do here all by myself?" she asked.

"Just relax, Jay. I know this all seems overwhelming, but you'll be fine. There's a buffet in the back, you can go in and get something to eat. Desiree and Rena should be arriving any minute, so keep an eye out for them. My interview should only last thirty minutes or so, and then I'll come find you. Oh, and here," she said, shoving two brown tickets into Jay's hand. "Text Rena and let her know Desiree has a booth in the Brown section of the loft."

"She gets a booth? Asked Jay.

"Yes," replied Jenna. "But new designers are not allowed on the floor when the buyers arrive. A stagehand will meet them in the loading area, and the ticket will let them know where her booth is and how to set it up. You need to hold onto the other brown ticket, because it's the only way for you to gain access into the showrooms, so don't lose it. One more thing, this event is very important, Jay, so please don't mess this up."

"Just give me the ticket, Jenna! You act like I have no sense. I know what to do." Jay walked off annoyed; she hated when her sister spoke down to her. As soon as she started making her way to the buffet station, her cell phone beeped with a text message; Rena and Desiree had arrived and were entering the parking lot. Jay was relieved to know they were here. The showroom was getting more and more crowded, and she was beginning to feel overwhelmed. By the time she found them, Mike and Carl had loaded the heavy items onto the dolly and left to explore New York City on their own.

"Hi, Jay isn't this exciting?" asked Rena. "We still have a lot of stuff to carry in; can you give us a hand?"

"I guess so," replied Jay, while handing one of the brown tickets to the stagehand. Rena stopped unloading her truck and nudged Desiree. They both laughed as they watched Jay pick up several garment bags until she found the lightest one and headed back toward the building.

Jay enjoyed being left in charge. "Come on, Desiree. Jenna said to register your bags as soon as you arrive, and when you're done, I'll sneak you inside so you can have a peak at the showroom; it's amazing."

As soon as Desiree finished the registration process, Jay kept her promise and managed to get them to the entrance of the showroom. "Jay, you were right; this really is amazing," said Rena. "I wonder where Desiree's booth will be."

Desiree's eyes gazed across the showroom as she watched some of the booths being set up. These designers had amazing props, and Desiree suddenly began to wonder if her props were good enough. "Jay, how come I don't see the Brown section anywhere on this map?" asked Desiree.

"I don't know," replied Jay. "Jenna just said to give them the brown ticket, and they will know what to do."

"Don't worry about it," said Rena. "Jenna has a lot of clout in this industry. I'm sure she got you a prime location."

"I don't know about that," replied Desiree. "You know she doesn't really like me."

"Maybe so," replied Rena. "But I know Jenna, and her ego would never allow her to call in a favor and then settle for anything less than the best."

Desiree laughed. "Good point," she said.

The show was about to begin so Jay quickly escorted Rena and Desiree out of the building.

Minutes later, the showroom began to fill with well-known designers and buyers. Wilfred was extremely pleased with the turnout. He moved to the front of the showroom to give his welcome speech. Standing on the platform of a small stage, he thanked everyone for coming, gave a brief history of the top designers who were in attendance, and invited the guests to partake of expensive champagne. Wilfred then introduced three of his hosts to the guests. The first host wore black pants, a white shirt, a black vest, and a gold tie, and he went straight to the section of the loft that was decorated with beautiful gold overtones. The next host came out dressed in black pants, a white shirt, a black vest, and a purple tie. This young man walked out and went to the section of the loft that had purple overtones. This format was repeated one final time with that host wearing a silver tie. It became obvious to Jay that the Gold, Silver, and Purple sections of the loft were reserved for the elite designers. The next set of men waiting to come forward also wore colored ties, and they quickly dispersed to the areas of the showroom that matched their ties. Jay saw red, blue, green, and even black ties. Missing from this well-coordinated presentation were brown ties; in fact, there was no mention of the Brown section at all in Wilfred's welcome speech.

After the speech the guests were released into the loft, and the stage was now set for some of the most dramatic displays of fashion to ever hit New York City. The harp player began her selection, while the photographers and journalists raced around looking for anything worthy of a story. Jay started to panic as she realized Jenna's interview was taking much longer than expected, and she had no idea where the Brown section of the loft was. To make matters worse, she realized she was still holding the garment bag that contained Desiree's mini evening bags. Jay decided not to wait around for Jenna; she needed to find the Brown section of the loft and get the remainder of Desiree's bags to the stagehands. Jay looked around and found a security guard who was happy to assist her. "Go straight to the back of the loft until you see a sign that says, 'restrooms.' The Brown section is right next to the bathrooms."

"There must be some mistake," Jay replied. "My sister knows Wilfred, and I remember her telling me our booth was up front; I think we were supposed to be in the Blue section."

"Sorry, Miss, but you asked me for the Brown section, and that's way in the back of the loft."

Jay was confused and decided she needed to call Jenna even if it meant interrupting her interview. After the first ring, the call went straight into voice mail. Jay was becoming frustrated, but after thirty minutes of roaming around the loft, she did manage to find the Brown section. The area was dark and isolated; she looked around and saw two large booths in the corner. There was a long table set up in the first booth; on top of the table were several small jars of paint, a few tiny brushes, and plain white t-shirts. The second booth had a large white table attached to it. Jay walked over to inspect the booth and found all of Desiree's props and her complete line of evening bags thrown on top of the table; she looked around in dismay, and quickly grabbed the arm of one of the stagehands passing by. "Excuse me, but what happened here? None of our stuff is set up, and the show has already started."

"We don't set up in the Brown section; you have to do that yourself," he replied before rushing off.

Jay stood there wondering what to do next. Jenna told her she had to stay in the booth, but she said nothing about setting it up. With Wilfred's show, now in full swing, Jay started to panic; but she was sure a drink would calm her down. As she struggled to get through the crowds of people, she found herself in front of a stage where a top designer was preparing to display her new line of bridal gowns. Standing only a few feet away from her was a model draped in a white, form-fitted bridal gown; the top of the gown had a sweetheart neckline while the bottom of the gown flowed elegantly to the floor. Suddenly, the music was cued, and a series of lights were released onto the stage. The main spotlight followed the model as she made her entrance. As she walked across the stage, the spotlight moved to the back of her dress, where her five-foot train was trimmed in diamonds. Jay gasped as the model walked past her; she wasn't sure if it was the gown that made the model look so beautiful, or if the model herself made the gown look so good. Either way, the designer struck gold with this design, and the crowd showed its approval with a standing ovation. Now Jay understood why there was so much security around this particular showcase. As the model exited the stage, she looked down at Jay and smiled. Jay was thrilled by the attention and she imagined herself wearing a gown like that on her wedding day. There was a woman standing next to her, and Jay became annoyed when the woman asked her a question.

"The bridal gowns are very beautiful, aren't they?" Jay ignored the kind stranger, but the woman was determined to get Jay's attention; she studied Jay for a few minutes before commenting on her engagement ring.

"Your ring is beautiful. When is your big day?" "Thank you," replied Jay without bothering to answer her question.

The woman moved closer toward her. "I see you have a brown ticket."

"What?" Jay replied, slightly annoyed.

"The brown ticket means you need to put your items on your table before it's too late. The buyers won't see anything that is not displayed with a ticket." Jay looked down and could not believe she was still holding Desiree's garment bag.

Jenna's words immediately rang in her ear, "Please Jay, don't mess this up." Jay turned and tried to find her way back to the Brown section, but by now the venue had opened up to the public, and there were twice as many people floating around. After more than thirty minutes, she was able to locate the Brown section, only to find it roped off. "Sorry, Miss, but this section is temporarily closed."

"What do you mean closed? I have a booth back there. Look, here is my ticket."

The security guard inspected the ticket, then said, "Okay, I can let you in, but you still have to wait a few minutes."

"Wait for what?" asked Jay.

"The private showing ended fifteen minutes ago, and Wilfred ordered all of the food and champagne to be moved to the Guest Lounge. The waiters are back there changing; they should only be a few more minutes."

Jay was about to walk away when she heard her phone ring. Relieved to see it was her sister calling, she quickly answered. "Jenna, where are you? This whole thing is a mess! Wilfred gave Desiree a booth way in the back, and no one bothered to set it up. You just left me here with all this stuff to do and no one to help!"

Jenna was remarkably calm. "Just put Desiree's bags on her table, Jay; you don't have to worry about setting anything up."

"But there's no room on the table; it's all covered with junk!"

"Then go ask them for another table. It's no big deal; I'll come find you as soon as I can."

"But, Jenna, the private showing is already over, how is Desiree going to get her review? No one is going to walk all the way back here!"

"I can't talk right now, Jay, I have to go."

When Jay heard the sudden click, she began to fume with anger. How dare her sister leave her with all this mess and act like it was no big deal? She marched up to the front of the showroom, where once again the crowd overtook her five-foot, two-inch frame. There was a great deal of excitement taking place, but she could not see what was happening. As she struggled to see over the crowd, Jay saw the kind woman who tried to speak to her earlier; she walked over to her. "What's happening?" Jay asked.

"Someone claims to have seen Miss Millie entering the building. Every photographer and writer in the fashion industry wants to interview her, and for some insane reason they believe she is in the building."

Jay was now ready to talk to the kind stranger. "My sister writes for a fashion magazine, and she did say Millie Enterprises was interested in a new line of bridal gowns; maybe she really did come."

The kind woman smiled at Jay. "I see you've done your homework, but I can assure you a woman of her caliber never attends these venues herself. However, I do believe one of her representatives is in the building, and that may be what all the fuss is about."

Jay stared intensely at the stranger. "How do you know so much?" she asked, but the woman never answered; instead, she looked down at the garment bag.

"I see you were not able to set up your booth; that's too bad since the buyers have already started to leave."

Jay began to panic. "You mean I missed everything?"

"You may still catch one or two of them, but you really must hurry."

"But I don't have a table," cried Jay. "Security closed off the Brown section, and all my stuff is in there."

"Then go over to registration and ask them for another table; as long as you have your ticket, they will give you a table."

Jay turned from the woman and rushed over to the registration booth, where she found a young man playing video games on his computer. "Where can I get another table?" she asked him.

"Where is your ticket?" Jay showed him the brown ticket. "That's way in the back, and those tickets only allow you to have one table."

"But I can't get into my area, and I need another table," she demanded.

"Well, then you have to go over and talk to security. I can't give the okay for anything in that section."

Jay was now frustrated and furious; she only agreed to work Desiree's booth so she could see the bridal gowns, and now she was missing everything. As she made her way toward the security office, her attention was drawn to the elevator, where two heavy set women were yelling for someone to find Wilfred. The crowd of photographers camped around them as the women threatened to shut the venue down if Wilfred did not find someone to unlock the door to their suite. Jay recognized the women right away. The two sisters inherited their grandfather's struggling shirt-and-tie business years ago and turned it into a successful empire with their over-the-top line of risqué shirts and wacky jeans. They were also the two people Jenna was scheduled to interview. The Cunningham sisters were known for their abusive manners, and they remained true to form as they hurled insults at Wilfred's staff. Now Jay understood why Jenna took so long to get back to her; she probably could not do the interview with the sisters locked out of their suite. Moments later Wilfred arrived on the scene and made a complete spectacle of himself by running up and down the halls screaming for Tiny to find the master key. Wilfred even managed to shed a few tears during his apology to the sisters; at that point he wanted nothing more than to get the Cunningham sisters to stop blasting his showcase.

As soon as the drama ended, the crowd spread out again. Jay turned around just in time to see Tiny hurry past her and into a door marked, "The Silver Room." Jay ran in right behind him and was amazed at what she saw. The room turned out to be a huge part of the loft that was decorated in silver with black and white trimmings. There were no crowds or photographers to fight through, and Jay was able to see most of the displays from where she stood. Instead of booths, these designers had actual scenes built for their displays. As her eyes continued to scan the room, Jay noticed a security guard staring at her, and she expected him to ask her to leave; but she had already decided not to be pushed around anymore. Marching up to a glass table that was next to him, she slammed the garment bag down on the table. "Keep an eye on these bags. I'll be right back," she ordered. Jay then turned and headed back out to the registration area.

The security guard watched quietly as two stagehands on their way to the Guest Lounge spotted the garment bag on the table. Believing they missed setting up one of the displays, they quickly emptied the garment bag and searched for the silver ticket that should have been attached to the items, but there was no registration ticket, no theme, and no props. With only a few buyers left in the building, time was running out, so they decided to stage the display themselves. Rushing into the stockroom, they returned with a dusty, old forest scene that had been sitting in the stockroom for years. Now all they could do was hope the mechanical parts of the prop still worked. They rolled the five-foot display of colorful trees and ceramic mountains into the venue and positioned the display in a corner. As they began cleaning the display, they tested the lights and moving streams of water; with everything working perfectly, they decided to display the larger evening bags on the ceramic part of the mountains, and they placed the smaller bags onto large rocks that stood alongside the waterfall. To ensure the bags would not be drowned out by the beauty of the scene itself, the men placed tiny colorful lights on a rotating disk and tucked them behind the trees; the reflection from the rotating lights slowly moved from the evening bags, onto the rocks, and then onto the waterfall. The dark corner of the showroom was transformed into a warm and serene scene.

As the two men walked away, one of them looked back at their work and said, "I hope that designer feels they got their money's worth, all nine thousand dollars of it!"

The designers in the Silver Room looked outside the window and counted the number of limousines left in the parking lot. With twelve limousines still parked outside, they reasoned there were at least twelve buyers left in the building. Wilfred's shows always attracted a good number of buyers, but this time several high-profile buyers responded to his invitation and Wilfred pulled out all the stops for them. Unlike the other parts of his show, the Silver Room was reserved for the elite buyers only; the press was not allowed in this room.

Moments later the elevator doors opened, and eleven buyers made their way into the Silver Room. Each of the buyers saw Desiree's evening bags, but none of them felt the bags were worthy of their attention. The buyers continued to breeze through the rest of the displays in the Silver Room and then made their exit out of the building. They spent a full six minutes viewing the fourteen displays. As soon as they left, Wilfred ordered the designers in the Silver Room to begin taking down their displays, but they protested. There was still one more limousine parked outside, which meant there was one more buyer still left in the building, and as long as that buyer had to exit through the Silver Room, the designers wanted to wait. No one knew who the last buyer was, and no one cared. Any buyer with access to Wilfred's Silver Room had the ability to put their product into the hands of millions of consumers, so they waited patiently.

When the doors of the service elevator opened, Sasha Montgomery stepped out and looked around. There were a few photographers and reporters still roaming around, and she hoped she could get past them without being noticed. Using the service elevator allowed her to stay under the radar; the press was foolish enough to dismiss her as unimportant simply because she rode in the elevator with the cleaning staff. Glancing at her watch, she decided to make time for the local designers; she wanted to see all of the designers' work, not just the ones who could afford to pay nine thousand dollars to showcase in the Silver Room. As she was about to enter the Blue Room, a reporter approached her. "Hello, Miss Montgomery. Are you filling in for your mother? Can you confirm whether or not she is in the building?" Sasha gave the reporter a cold stare before turning her back to him. She realized going into the Blue Room meant dealing with the press, so she turned and headed for the safety of the Silver Room. That reporter decided not to follow her since the Silver Room was off limits to the press, but another reporter was better prepared.

Barrington watched patiently as Sasha Montgomery made her way toward the Silver Room. "That's her," he confirmed to himself. "Sasha Montgomery, lead counsel for Millie Enterprises and Miss Millie's daughter." Barrington had spent several weeks researching the empire her mother built and was curious about the mother-daughter relationship that so many people wanted to know about. Knowing Sasha Montgomery was a fierce contender in the courtroom; Barrington wondered what she was like when she wasn't taking down one of her opponents. He also understood how she managed to stay under the radar of most photographers and reporters in the industry. Barrington slowly approached her. "Ms. Montgomery?" Sasha looked over her shoulder to see a handsome young man with a boyish grin smiling at her. "Hello, my name is Barrington. I am a freelance journalist."

Barrington held out his hand, but Sasha ignored his gesture and simply replied, "I don't give interviews," then she walked into the Silver Room, leaving Barrington standing at the doorway.

Not easily defeated, Barrington charmed his way into the kitchen and walked out with a serving tray full of appetizers. He shook open a linen napkin, placed it over his arm, and went into the Silver Room in search of Sasha Montgomery.

It only took Sasha a few minutes to realize she was out of her comfort zone in reviewing the designers' work. Having spent most of her time in the courtroom, she had no idea what to write on their review cards; in her opinion, everything she saw was breathtaking. Sasha wanted to spend a few minutes with each designer, but the handsome, young journalist derailed her good intentions. "Ms. Montgomery, would you care for a shrimp puff or radish ball?" Sasha was clearly annoyed, but Barrington received it warmly. Looking down at his tray, he said, "Honestly, Ms. Montgomery, I have no idea what's on this tray. I was just told to serve it."

Sasha noticed the awkward way Barrington held the serving tray and the linen napkin carelessly thrown over his shoulder. "The napkin does not belong on your shoulder, and you're not holding the tray correctly." she said.

Barrington smiled and again extended his hand. "It's nice to meet you, Ms. Montgomery. I admit I am out of place, acting as a server, but I can assure you, I am a very good journalist."

"Are you looking for a job, Barrington?" she asked.

"No, Ma'am, I am strictly freelance. I was hoping you would grant me an interview, maybe even one with your mother?"

"That's not possible, Barrington; as I already told you,

I do not give interviews, now if you will excuse me."

Sasha turned her back to him and started to walk away, but Barrington's next comment stopped her in her tracks. "Nice job on the runway, Ms. Montgomery. I don't know too many lawyers who could look that beautiful modeling."

Sasha looked back at Barrington, and for a moment she was at a loss for words. Walking back toward him she asked, "So what happens now, Barrington? You threaten to publish my photo in some newspaper unless I agree to give you an interview?"

Barrington reached into his pocket and handed her an SD card. "This is the clip of you modeling the diamond studded wedding gown; it's my only copy, and it's yours to keep. Consider it a token of trust, and one day when you're ready to tell your story; I hope you will remember me. I want you to know you can trust me, Ms. Montgomery."

Sasha stared intently at him; if he were looking for a job, she would have hired him on the spot, but Barrington wanted much more. He wanted to know what it was like growing up with London's biggest fashion icon for a mother, and Sasha never gave anyone permission to enter into her life, past or present. "Barrington," she said. "I can't imagine our paths ever crossing again, but if they ever do, I promise to give you an interview on one condition."

"Anything, Ms. Montgomery, just name it!"

Sasha walked up close to him and whispered, "Never ever refer to me as ma'am; I am only twenty-eight years old."

Barrington blushed. "Sorry, I was just trying to be polite. Let me give you my card," he said while struggling to balance the serving tray in one hand. Sasha held the tray for him. She watched him carefully as he retrieved his business card from a very expensive case and handed it to her. "I'll take that tray back now," he said. "I promised the young lady in the kitchen I would return it right away."

Sasha opened her pocketbook and placed his business card inside. "It was very nice meeting you, Barrington."

"The pleasure was all mine, Miss Montgomery."

With her flight back to London less than two hours away, there was little time for her to view the displays. Sasha hurried past the designers who stood by hoping for a few minutes of her time; she was about to make her exit when a ray of colorful lights coming from a waterfall caught her attention. Sasha could never resist a waterfall, and she wondered what the designer was showcasing. As she made her way to the corner of the venue, a purple colored evening bag caught her attention. The bag was cut in the shape of a triangle, with a thin strap tied to one side and scrolls of silk flowers sewn in the middle. There was a second bag that looked identical to the first one. At first Sasha was confused by the duplication, but when she held both bags, she realized one bag was made using a very high-end fabric; the second bag held all of the beauty of the first, but the designer used a more moderately priced fabric to create the same look. Sasha appreciated the sensitivity of the designer. Having grown up in a wealthy family, she was always conscious about the less privileged. With her mother's company only catering to high-end consumers, Sasha thought this designer could help Millie Enterprises tap into a new market of consumers. She looked around for the silver ticket that should have been set up with the display, but she could not find one. Sasha looked at her map and realized not only was there no silver ticket, but this display was set up in the Cunningham sisters' reserved spot. Sasha opened up one of the evening bags and found a label inside. "Hunter Designs" was elegantly stitched inside the fabric. Sasha searched the display but could not find a bio on the designer, and there was no company information or even a host to give her information on the designer. Sasha checked her watch and realized she was running behind schedule. Since it was customary for the designers to give away samples of their products to interested buyers, she assumed it was okay to take the two evening bags. Once she got back to London, she would have someone from their marketing department contact the designer. Sasha smiled as she made her way past the designers and hurried outside to her waiting limousine.

Finally, she was able to relax. Sasha kicked off her heels and lay back in her seat. It felt good being away from all the people in the fashion industry who were trying to make a name for themselves. Coming to this event served no real purpose. Sasha knew her mother had no intention of signing any new designers, but these venues were good for publicity, and nothing sold more of Miss Millie's designs than the hype that surrounded them.

It took the driver one hour to make his way through the New York City traffic and into JFK Airport. After checking in, Sasha went straight to the lounge for first-class travelers. There was still a few minutes left before passengers could board the plane, so she called home and gave her mother a quick update.

"Sasha, darling, how did it go?"

"Hi, Mom, the showcase was very nice, nothing to get excited about, but it was very nice."

"Well, tell me about the show the Cunningham sisters put on. I heard they hired live models, and an artist was going to paint designs on their shirts as they walked across the stage; it was supposed to be a showstopper."

"I'm not sure what happened to them," replied Sasha. "Another designer was set up in their spot; maybe they didn't attend this year."

Miss Millie was quiet for a few minutes before replying to her daughter. "Sasha, dear, the Cunningham sisters book the same space every year. Are you telling me you missed the biggest attraction at Wilfred's showcase?"

Sasha hated disappointing her mother, but this time she had. "Mom, you know how I hate coming to these events; you really should have sent someone else."

"Well, did you at least enjoy yourself while you were there? Were there any nice men around?"

Sasha chuckled. "I worked on a case that's going to court in a few weeks, shopped in the Village, and ate in my room. Did they have a display of single men at Wilfred's showcase? If so, I'd better get back there," she laughed.

"Oh, Sasha," replied Miss Millie. "I just don't want you to end up alone."

"Mom, you worry too much. Listen, I have an idea. I will have someone from our office get the showcase sent to us on media, and then we can find out what happened to the Cunningham sisters, okay?"

"All right, honey, have a safe trip home. I love you."

"I love you too, Mom." Sasha hung up her phone and heard the call for passengers flying first class to begin boarding the plane. After she settled into her seat, she began thinking about the Cunningham sisters. Her mother was right, their attraction was one of the biggest events scheduled; it did seem strange that they would not have shown up, but she was certain the sisters were not there. Now all she had to do was prove to her mother that she did not let the biggest attraction at the venue slip past her.

Sasha reached up and pushed the light over her seat. A flight attendant responded immediately. "Can I have a cup of hot water for my tea?"

"Sure what kind of tea can I bring you?"

"Just the water please, I have my own tea bag."

The attendant came back with a cup of hot water and placed it front of her. Sasha took a teabag from a wooden case and placed it in her cup. The scent of raspberry quickly filled her cup, and she began to relax. As soon as she reached back into her pocketbook to put back the wooden tea box, she saw Barrington's business card and she felt relieved. Barrington was there covering the showcase, and he would know what happened to the Cunningham sisters. The passengers in coach were still boarding, so she decided to give him a call, but her call went straight to his voice mail. Rather than leave a message, she decided to send him a text message. With Barrington being so young, she reasoned texting was probably his major line of communicating anyway.

Within minutes, a text came back to her. "Yes, Sasha, I can get the story for you. Call me and let me know when I can come to London." Sasha was not sure she read his response correctly; he could not possibly think she would expect him to travel to London to deliver the story.

She immediately replied, "No need to come to London, you can just send me a media kit."

Barrington replied, "You said if our paths ever crossed again you would grant me an interview. I believe our paths are crossing now?"

Sasha was shocked. She made that promise believing the two of them would never meet again, but he was right; their paths were crossing, and now she would have to keep her word.

"Okay," she replied. "But what information I share with you will be based on how good your information is." Sasha hit the send button; then she waited. The Cunningham sisters were one of the biggest attractions in the showcase, if Barrington was as good a journalist as he claimed to be, he would bring back the full story on them without her having to ask for it. Sasha then sent another text, "Barrington I have one more request, I need you to track down a designer for me; her name is Desiree Hunter. I don't have any other information on her, except I know she had a display in the Silver Room."

Barrington's reply was swift. "Consider it done."

When Mike and Carl pulled into the loading zone, they found Rena upset and Desiree in tears. "What happened?" asked Mike.

"We don't know yet," replied Rena. "When we went inside to pack up Desiree's booth, we found her evening bags thrown on top of a table in the back of the loft. One of the workers inside said they did not have an order to set up her booth, so her bags just sat there." Mike sighed, and then he walked to the back of the truck and began helping Carl load the props back into the truck.

When Jay came strolling out of the building, Rena yelled at her. "Jay, what happened in there? How come Desiree's booth was not set up?"

"It wasn't my fault," Jay yelled. "They gave Desiree a brown ticket, and no one told me they don't set up booths for people with brown tickets."

"She had a blue ticket," yelled Rena. "Jenna gave us the paperwork and everything so stop lying!"

"I'm not lying," said Jay. "I heard Jenna on the phone myself; she asked Wilfred to change Desiree's booth at the last minute. Wilfred got mad and started yelling at her, and then he changed all her tickets to brown ones." Jay looked over at Desiree. "I'm sorry no one saw your stuff, Desiree. The security guards blocked off that area, and your stuff just sat on the table, but this was not my fault."

Rena stood in disbelief as she realized Jay was telling the truth. Whatever happened in that building happened without Jay's knowledge. Rena pulled out her cell phone and tried calling Jenna, but each time she called, she got Jenna's voicemail.

"Come on, Rena, let's go," said Mike.

"Mike, I can't believe Jenna did this; how could she be so cruel?"

"Don't jump to conclusions. At least wait until you talk to Jenna and find out what happened," said Mike.

But Rena did not need to talk to Jenna; she knew Jenna ruined this opportunity for Desiree. Hurting Desiree was one thing, but Jenna made a fool of her too, and Rena was not taking it lightly.

As Mike drove off, he listened as Rena tried to comfort Desiree. "Desiree, I know you're upset, but you have to pull yourself together. We don't want your mom or the baby to see you so upset. Mike, honey, can we stop and get some water or something so Desiree has a little time to calm down?"

Mike pulled into the parking lot of a convenience store and got out. He returned with two cups of coffee; he handed one to Carl and placed the other one in his cup holder, then he handed Rena two bottles of water. As the four of them sat in the truck, Mike watched Rena from his rearview mirror; she had so much compassion for Desiree that it made him sick to his stomach. If only she would share some of that compassion with him.

When they drove back to the hotel to pick up Mrs.

Hunter and Gabriel; Mike and Carl loaded a few items into Rena's truck and sent them back to Atlanta, while they headed back to Wilfred's event to retrieve the heavier items.

Mike was happy Mrs. Hunter made the trip; that meant Rena had help driving and he could avoid being around Rena, as she comforted Desiree.

Meanwhile, Carl silently hoped he would not run into Jenna. He wasn't sure what happened to Desiree's showcase, but he knew Jenna well enough to know, this was no accident.

CHAPTER FIFTEEN

Darlene just finished typing Pastor Lee's notes from the sermon, when a deliveryman entered the church's basement lobby. Darlene got up to greet him. "I have a delivery for a Darlene Jones."

Darlene was stunned. "I'm Ms. Jones."

"Okay, then just sign here," he said before handing the large vase of flowers to her.

Darlene was signing for the flowers when Pastor Lee entered the lobby. "Oh, did I miss your birthday or something?"

"No, it's not my birthday, but someone did send me flowers; it must be from one of our vendors," she replied.

Pastor Lee laughed. "Vendors don't send those expensive flowers, Darlene; you must have a secret admirer." Darlene gave him a doubtful look before pulling the card from the plastic wrap. Darlene read the card out loud, "'Ms. Jones, many thanks for all of your time and patience. I look forward to meeting you in person, signed, Barrington.' These are from that reporter who's been calling here all week," she said. "I told you about him."

"Well, what does he want?" asked Pastor Lee while going through his mail.

"He wants to talk to you about your investment in Hunter Designs. He says he was hired to locate the designer, but his questions seem strange; he's asking about your past."

Pastor Lee stopped sorting his mail and looked up at her. "You know, I heard Katherine Johnson has been complaining about this young man too. It seems he has been tap dancing on everyone's nerves all week. Why don't you set him up with an appointment? I should be able to see him sometime next week."

"I tried to set up an appointment Pastor, but he insists on seeing you immediately. He's a bit arrogant and has already booked his flight here."

Pastor Lee looked concerned. "Let me have his number." Darlene handed him a piece of paper with Barrington's phone number on it. "I'll be in my office, and you'd better hold my calls. It sounds like this young man is eager to talk."

Darlene could not remember the last time she received flowers. While it was true Barrington drove everyone crazy, with all of his questions, he certainly had excellent taste and spared no expense with the flowers he sent. With all of the excitement the flowers generated, she forgot to give Pastor Lee one other important message. The pink message slip fell to the ground as Darlene placed the beautiful assortment of flowers on her desk. As she got up to admire the arrangement, she stepped on the pink message slip that read, "Hello, I bet you never thought this day would come, but it has arrived. Please call me....this is Courtney."

Darlene smiled, she could not believe how those flowers changed her day; she grabbed her pocketbook and decided to take an early lunch.

When Pastor Lee came out of his office, he could not find Darlene and he did not trust sharing his news with anyone else; at least not yet, so he found Desiree's phone number and called her. Desiree agreed to come back to church that afternoon, believing that Pastor Lee just wanted to give her a pep talk and encourage her not to give up on her dream; but when he asked her to bring her mother along, Desiree knew something more serious was taking place.

Later that afternoon, Desire arrived at the church with her mother and son; they went downstairs to the church office and knocked. When Pastor Lee opened the door, she was surprised to see the Marshalls, who were the church's legal team and Katherine Johnson, waiting for her arrival.

"Have a seat, Desiree; we have some exciting news to share with you." Desiree had pits in the bottom of her stomach. She handed Gabriel over to her mother and sat down. Pastor Lee spoke first, "It seems that a young journalist by the name of Barrington has been driving my secretary crazy all week and today I discovered why." Desiree kept silent as she searched the faces in the room, hoping to get a sense of what was going on. It was only when Katherine reached over and touched her hand that she knew everything was okay. "Desiree, were any of your bags missing after the show?" asked Pastor Lee.

"Yes," replied Desiree. "Two of my evening bags are still missing. I believe Jay took them; she claims she doesn't have them. I don't believe her, but so many things went wrong with my showcase, I guess anyone could have taken them. I'm really upset because those were my best evening bags and one of them was quite expensive."

Pastor Lee smiled. "It seems there was a woman by the name of Sasha Montgomery in the showroom. Apparently, she did not know the correct protocol for obtaining a designer's work. From what I learned, it is not unusual for a designer to give away free samples of their merchandise to an interested buyer. I believe that's why Sasha Montgomery thought it was okay to take the bags with her. Anyway, I can confirm, she is the one who took your bags, not Jay. Your missing bags are currently in London."

Desiree smiled. "A real buyer liked my bags? How did she even see them? My booth was never set up."

"We don't know how it happened," answered Pastor Lee. "But according to Barrington, the journalist who was hired to track you down; your evening bags ended up on a nine-thousand-dollar display in the Silver Room."

"No way Pastor! I saw what the Silver Room looked like. Those designers had unbelievable displays and I barely had enough props to set up the few bags that were good enough to make it into the show; you remember me telling you some of my bags were rejected during the registration process? And now you're telling me some of my bags made it into the Silver Room? Who set my bags up?"

Pastor Lee laughed. He knew this was God's mighty hand at work; even Barrington said he was floored when he uncovered the events that led to Hunter Designs ending up in the Cunningham Sisters' section while they were locked out of their suite.

"I know this all sounds a bit overwhelming Desiree, but I can assure you, this was no accident. You have heard me preach on God's favor many times before. When He is ready to release His favor, it surpasses all understanding!"

Desiree leaped out of her seat and ran into Miss Katherine's open arms. "Ms. Katherine, we did it! We did it!"

"Now hold on, Desiree, I don't want you to get too excited," warned Pastor Lee. "We have not actually heard from Ms. Sasha Montgomery herself. I received this information from Barrington, but he seems to be able to back up everything he has told me about meeting Sasha Montgomery. At this point, the buyer has only expressed an interest in meeting with you. Barrington told me they were waiting to hear from us; I called them earlier today, expecting to just leave a message, but a young man answered the phone and confirmed everything. I took the liberty of inviting the Marshalls here, and they have graciously agreed to act as your legal advisors."

"Thank you," said Desiree as she ran up and hugged the Marshalls. "I can't believe this is really happening! Who did you say this buyer was?" asked Desiree.

Betty Marshall now stood up. "That's the main reason we are here, Desiree. Your bags did not end up in the hands of an ordinary buyer. The woman who took your bags works for Millie Enterprises, one of the largest distributors of high-end merchandise in London. They hold their own in other countries too."

Desiree turned to her mother and asked, "Did she say Millie Enterprises?"

Desiree's mother had tears in her eyes. "Is this true Pastor? Someone from Millie Enterprises wants to meet my daughter?"

"Yes," replied Pastor Lee. "But we must move quickly, they want to send their people to meet with us and if all goes well, Desiree could be on her way to London in a few short weeks."

Pastor Lee then looked over at Desiree and said, "I do believe the Lord has blessed you kindly."

CHAPTER SIXTEEN

Desiree still could not believe how fast everything happened. It was early Sunday morning; Desiree looked down at her son and smiled. After countless phone calls, several, very long meetings and loads of paperwork, the Marshalls were able to secure a contract for her with Millie Enterprises. Desiree picked Gabriel up and started spinning him around in circles. "This is it, honey, today we leave for London! Now listen, we have a very long plane ride ahead of us, and mommy needs you to be a good boy." Gabriel laughed and wanted to keep playing, but Desiree kissed his forehead, and then placed him in his stroller. As she walked around her empty apartment, she laughed at how little she had to pack. A knock on the door caused her to jump. Desiree looked through the peephole, saw Mr. Dave and opened the door.

"Are you ready to go, kid?"

"Yes, I am," replied Desiree as she handed over her keys.

"Come on, I'll take your suitcases out for you."

Desiree almost forgot how sweet Mr. Dave was when he was not complaining about her rent being late. Desiree picked up two envelopes and handed them to him. "Here is this month's rent, and this is the address where you can send my security deposit."

Mr. Dave took the envelopes from her. "Desiree, I am so sorry for everything that happened to you and your friend that night, and I'm glad your boyfriend was not responsible for hurting anyone."

"I'm sorry too, Mr. Dave. I know I've been a lot of trouble."

"Nonsense, you were a young mother trying to make it in this mean and cold world. It wasn't easy, kid, but you made it. Here, I have something for you." Mr. Dave held out his hand and dropped an inexpensive necklace into Desiree's hand. The necklace had a black shoe, a boot, a sneaker and a sandal hanging from it.

"What's this?" she asked.

"Desiree, you are starting a new journey, on the path God has laid out for you. Knowing when to change shoes will help keep you on your path."

Desiree laughed and said, "Change shoes?"

Mr. Dave remained serious as he spoke. "Everyone has a path in this life, but many of us never find it. You gave your life to God and now He is directing your path. Mr. Dave began explaining each shoe, one by one. You see this pretty black shoe? This black shoe commands a lot of attention and is cleverly designed to take you off your path; be very careful of black shoes on your path. Now, this boot represents spiritual warfare. It prepares your feet for battle. The sneaker is very important; it represents your ability to run your race. No matter how many times you may fall, get back up. Stay in the race at all times! And when life gets too hard, remember God has provided a bridge to help get you over difficult times. You can find rest and safety on the bridge, but don't get stuck there; there are already too many shoes on the bridge. Finally, when you reach your destination, look back at the many people too afraid to leave the bridge and offer your sandal as a token of encouragement. And no matter how successful you become, always remember the people God placed on your path. It was their obedience to God that brought forth your blessing. We all have a path to walk Desiree, but none of us can walk it alone." Desiree had tears in her eyes. "Mr. Dave, that was beautiful."

"Come on," he replied. "Let's get you outside."

Desiree's mother was just pulling into a parking space when they came out of the alley. Mrs. Hunter got out of the car and immediately went to the trunk as she waved to Desiree to hurry along. Desiree never remembered seeing her mother so happy and so peaceful. She carefully studied her mother, who was dressed in a white linen pantsuit with navy-blue sandals and a blue-and-white polka-dot scarf. It was obvious she had been to the hair and nail salon. Taking a deep breath, Desiree walked over and helped her mother load the car while Mr. Dave got down on one knee and played with Gabriel. When the last suitcase was loaded, Desiree walked over to Mr. Dave; he lifted himself up and stood before her. "Goodbye, Desiree," he said, holding out his hand. Desiree gently pushed his hand away and hugged him. "Goodbye, Mr. Dave."

Moments later the car started, and they drove off. Gabriel turned and waved goodbye to Mr. Dave, and Mr. Dave waved back.

Mike was reading his Sunday newspaper while Rena cleaned up. Today Pastor Lee was making the official announcement about Desiree and her contract with Millie Enterprises. Rena stopped cleaning and stood quietly as the thought of her friend being so far away sank in. "Hey, honey, you okay?" asked Mike while placing his arms around his wife's waist. "You miss her already, don't you?"

"I don't know what I'm feeling right now. I know this is a dream come true for her. I just wish Desiree could have stayed here. London is so far away."

Mike pulled Rena toward him. "You are always worrying about her; she's going to be fine."

"I know," said Rena. "I just can't believe she's not going to be here for the opening of the community center or at church anymore." Mike watched his wife's sadness from the corner of his eye. He was glad Desiree was gone; maybe now things would change and Rena could focus more on their marriage. Rena reached out and took his hand. "Mike, I'm so sorry I've been so preoccupied with Desiree. I know it wasn't fair to you." Mike finished his juice, but he did not respond. All this time he believed Rena was oblivious to the amount of time she spent with Desiree, only to hear her admit she was aware of it all along. He was hurt, but he would do anything to avoid an argument so he suppressed his feelings. "You know, Mike, we're in line to have some of our prayers answered too."

"I know," said Mike, fearing this conversation was leading into another episode of his wife not being able to conceive.

Rena looked at her husband. "You know, last night I started thinking about Pastor Lee's sermon, the one where he said people get frustrated waiting on God to answer their prayers, and not realizing God is waiting for them to get into the right place to receive it."

"I remember that sermon too," replied Mike. "But we're in a good place; we own our own home, I have a good job, and I know you will make a great mother."

Rena smiled as she loaded the dishwasher. "Thank you, honey, but Pastor Lee was referring to maturity. He said it's like the five year old child who wants a Mountain bike for his birthday, but his father knows he can't handle that level of responsibility yet. It doesn't mean God doesn't want to answer our prayers, it just means we have to be mature enough to handle what we are asking for."

Mike grabbed Rena by the waist and kissed her. They had so few moments like this. "Listen, before we leave for church, I want to run something past you," said Mike. "James Marshall and I are heading up the boys' youth group, and Pastor Lee asked us to give them a ten-minute introduction on what the youth ministry is about. Since these boys only seem to care about football, I decided to use that as a metaphor for their training."

Rena hopped up on the kitchen stool and folded her hands on the table. "Okay, teacher, I'm ready. You have two minutes to hold my attention."

Mike laughed and said, "I'm going to need a little more time than that."

"Okay," replied Rena. "But remember we're talking about a group of boys, all under the age of twelve."

Mike went into the bedroom and brought out the Bible and his football and placed them on the floor. He positioned himself for his audience, cleared his throat, and began. "Welcome to the community youth program; I am Mr. Mike Rollins; you can call me Mr. Mike. I will be assisting Mr. Marshall in training you all to become God's soldiers. Does anyone here like football?"

"I do, I do," cheered Rena while throwing both hands in the air.

"Good," replied Mike. "Anyone joining this team must want to play for the Light Team; our opponent is the Dark Team. Our mission is to get the ball into the end zone. The end zone is where all of your blessings are. Now I want you to think of God as your head coach in life. Keep your focus on Him at all times and He will get you into the end zone. Now, the Dark Team has all kinds of tricks and traps to keep you from getting into the end zone, but your head coach has already conquered the Dark Team; He just needs you to complete the plays. Everything you need to defeat The Dark Team is right here in this book." Mike held the Bible up high in the air while his foot held the football in place on the floor. "We have one very important rule. You are never, ever to attempt to defeat the Dark Team with your own strength, their plays and tactics can only be defeated by knowing what is in this book! The first thing Mr. Marshall and I will teach you is how to put on your full armor. In football we put on our helmet to protect our head, and the same rule applies here. The Dark Team wants to control your thinking, so your helmet of salvation is the first piece of armor we will train you to put on.

"Now imagine you all are on the football field. The play is made, and the Dark Team is charging at you. They look strong and scary. Your head coach is giving you instructions on how to overcome them, but you can't hear Him because your spiritual vision is blocked by what you see with your natural eye. The quarterback is about to get sacked, but his training kicks in, and he quickly passes the ball to the running back; now the Dark Team is after the running back. The enemy doesn't care about the football; he just wants to stop you from getting into the end zone. The Dark Team is closing in on the running back, the head coach is calling for the blockers to assist, but the blockers are not there. They were called to specific positions, but they decided to do their own thing. The Dark Team now has a clear path to the running back and manages to take him down. What we are left with is another young man who had his future stolen by the enemy. Mr. Marshall and I plan to win back our youth who are already playing on the Dark Team and we need you to help us. Now the head coach wants me to ask you if you are willing to be trained to serve on His team. Will you trust Him to get you into the end zone? Will you follow Him and stay the course?" Mike picked up the football and placed it under his arm, then he held the Bible in his other hand and began pacing the kitchen floor, pretending to speak to the boys on the bench. "Are you ready to make your choice? Where are our doctors? Our engineers? Our pilots? I'm looking around this room, and I see entrepreneurs, teachers, strong and responsible future fathers. You can do this, and we are here to show you how!"

Rena jumped down from the stool and clapped feverishly. "Mike, that was amazing! I love it, and Pastor Lee will love it too!" Rena ran up to him and gave her husband a hug and kissed him on the cheek. "I am so proud of you."

"Thanks honey. I'll run this by Pastor Lee today." Mike felt good. Rena was his best support system, and she was also the only one who would be honest enough to tell him the truth. He hoped Pastor Lee would approve, but even if he did not, his wife said she was proud of him, and that was really all that mattered to him. "Come on, Rena, we better get going; you know the service will be packed today."

A half hour later, Mike returned to the kitchen to check on Rena. It always took her so long to get ready, and he was anxious to get to church so he could meet with Pastor Lee.

"Oh, Mike! Listen to what my horoscope says." Mike stopped suddenly and took a deep breath; he hated the horoscopes and encouraged Rena to stay away from it, but as usual she never listened to him. "My horoscope says something I am waiting for is about to happen! This is it, Mike; this is God's confirmation. We've been trying to have a baby for so long, and now the horoscope says it will happen soon."

Mike pulled the paper from her. "I told you before, Rena, leave these horoscopes alone. That may be the reason our prayers are blocked."

"Oh, don't be ridiculous, Mike; everyone reads horoscopes."

Mike gave her a frustrated look. "How many times does the Bible tell us to go to our horoscope for confirmation, Rena?" Rena was quiet. As usual, Mike was shooting down her dream again. If he wasn't discouraging her from starting her catering business, he was telling her there was nothing wrong with waiting to have a baby.

"You are always criticizing me, Mike. Maybe you just don't want a baby."

"You know that's not true, Rena."

Rena threw the rest of the newspaper down and stormed past her husband. "I'm going to get ready," she said. Mike picked up the newspaper and put it in the garbage. He knew this day would be tough on his wife; between her still not being able to conceive and Desiree leaving, he realized the best thing he could do for her, was to stay out of her way.

Rena stood in the mirror, replaying Mike's crushing comments. How dare he blame her for their prayers not being answered; she thought for a few minutes before deciding it was time to throw the dirt back in Mike's face. She reached into the drawer and pulled out their checkbook, then headed downstairs and into the living room. "Honey, you know we haven't paid our tithes to the church in over a year. Why don't you write them a check?"

Mike spoke calmly. "I told you, Rena, we have to take care of the back taxes, and that loan I took out from the credit union came due. We just can't tithe right now." Mike knew she was trying to push his buttons; he picked up a magazine and tried to avoid eye contact with her.

"Okay, honey but you know what the Bible says about robbing God."

Mike threw the magazine on the couch and quickly walked out of the living room. Rena chuckled. Feeling vindicated, she headed back upstairs and went into the bedroom closet where she searched for an outfit to wear to church.

When she was finally dressed, she came downstairs to find Mike already outside sitting in his jeep. Rena started to feel bad; their morning started out so nicely and turned ugly in a matter of minutes. This has to stop she thought, as she made her way out of the house and into the jeep. The only problem was, she did not know what to do with her anger.

They rode in silence for the full twenty minutes it took to get to Jenna's house. When Mike pulled into Jenna's driveway, he looked at Rena and said, "I still can't believe Jenna and Jay are coming to church today."

"Believe it," replied Rena. "Desiree left letters for me, Jay, and Carl with Pastor Lee. I told Jay I would bring her letter to her, but Jay believes Desiree left her some money, and she insisted on coming to church to get it herself."

"Great," replied Mike. "So if there's no money in Jay's envelope, I get to drive three angry women home."

"Don't start with me, Mike," warned Rena.

Jay came out first; she greeted Mike and Rena with a cheerful hello as she climbed into the truck. Jenna emerged minutes later and climbed into the truck without saying a word to anyone. Mike was already exhausted; the tension between him and Rena was nothing new, but the tension between Rena and Jenna made everyone around them uncomfortable.

When they finally arrived at church, Jay began rushing them inside. "Come on, the car is parked, now let's get inside. I don't know how much money Desiree left me, but I plan to spend it all on my wedding."

Rena looked over at Jay. "I don't think Desiree has any money, at least not yet. That reporter confirmed your story on how her bags ended up in that room. Desiree probably just wants to say thank you."

"Well, she better had left something for my sister," replied Jenna. "I would hate to think I got up this early on a Sunday morning for nothing."

"Well, you didn't have to come," replied Rena. "You're probably only here to see Carl anyway. It's all about Carl with you, isn't it?"

Jenna snatched off her shades and was about to unleash a verbal attack on Rena when Mike cut in. "Ladies, please let's not do this right now."

"Well, your wife started it," replied Jenna. "She better leave me alone."

As they made their way into the church, Pastor Lee patiently waited for their arrival. "Good morning, Pastor. I'm sorry we're late," said Mike.

"Well, I'm glad you all made it here so early. I see we have two new faces this morning?"

Rena smiled. "Pastor, these are my friends Jenna and Jay Livingston."

"Welcome," replied Pastor Lee. "I do hope you will stay for our service." Jenna and Jay ignored the invitation. Jay stared down at the two envelopes in his hand while Jenna's attention was drawn to Carl, who was standing in a corner talking to a very attractive woman. Pastor Lee took one of the envelopes and handed it to Jay, then he turned to Rena and said "Desiree left this for you. She said to be careful about bending the envelope; there are pictures of Gabriel inside. Now if you all will excuse me, Mike and I have a meeting this morning."

As Mike prepared to leave, Rena pulled him aside and whispered in his ear, "You're going to blow him away with your introduction; it's really good."

Jay's hands were shaking with excitement; she tore the envelope open and read the note. "Dear Jay, I am sorry I could not do this in person, but I do owe you an apology. I thought you took my bags after the showcase, and I am sorry for accusing you. I wish you love and happiness on your upcoming marriage. Love, Desiree."

Jay's heart sank; she crumbled up the note and started to complain, "Desiree is so ungrateful! If it weren't for me, she would not be sitting on a pile of money right now; she better send me a postdated check or something!"

Rena gave Jay a scornful look, but Jay didn't seem to care. Jenna also became upset and decided to voice her opinion, "You see, Rena, that's why I hate doing favors for people. If it weren't for me, Desiree would be right back in the slums where she belongs." Jenna then watched as the young woman talking to Carl began flirting with him, and she decided she had seen enough. Jenna picked up her bag and scarf and stormed out of the church, with Jay following right behind her.

Rena sat in the pew alone for several minutes, before Carl and Darlene joined her. A few minutes later, Mike returned with Pastor Lee, who was still smiling. "Rena, you were right. Your husband's introduction blew me away." Pastor Lee patted Mike on the back. "Well, family, I have to get ready for today's service. As you can imagine, Desiree's news has the congregation very excited, but it has also left the church with a few vacant positions. Oh, and by the way, Carl, I heard what you did for Desiree and Gabriel. That was very generous of you to give them your home. I'm glad you were there for them, thank you."

James and Betty Marshall relaxed in their customized home that sat on twenty-two acres in the upscale Atlanta area. James Marshall smiled as he pushed the newspaper toward his wife. "This is it, Betty, right there on the front page of the business and fashion section. Millie Enterprises to sign newcomer Desiree Hunter in a trial run of elegant evening bags."

Betty smiled at her husband. "You did it again, honey; your negotiating skills landed Desiree a nice contract."

But James Marshall was troubled. "I don't know, Betty; something is not right with this sudden change of events. We closed this deal several days ago, and now Sasha Montgomery wants a meeting with us?"

Betty Marshall placed a cup of tea in front of her husband. "You know, honey, I checked out this Sasha Montgomery; she is usually brought in to handle the more difficult cases and never gets involved in these small transactions."

James put his cup down and began rubbing his head. Betty signaled for the maid to come and clear the table, she could tell her husband was stressed, so she walked over and began rubbing his back. "Do you think the church will agree to our demands?" she asked.

James looked at her with a prideful grin. "They have no choice; either they give us what we want, or we stop representing Desiree, and with Sasha Montgomery scheduled to arrive here in two days, Pastor Lee is not in a position to say no. We have the church right where we want them. We should really get going; the service will start soon, and I want to catch Pastor Lee as soon as it ends."

Pastor Lee stood near the door smiling as the choir sang, "Oh, What a Mighty God We Serve." This day was so special; he loved being able to witness God's blessing on one of his members. Once the choir fell silent, the congregation waited for him to enter.

"Family, friends, and visitors welcome. I am Pastor Lee. Before we begin our service today, I would like to share some exciting news with you all. Desiree Hunter has left the church and is on her way to London to begin working with Millie Enterprises. Let us all take a moment to pray for her safety as well as those who are traveling with her. I also have an update on the Johnson sisters. As many of you know, the Johnson sisters have been fighting off a foreclosure on their home for several months now. The church has done all we could to help them, and today I regret to inform you that the bank moved ahead and foreclosed on the property last week." Many of the church members gasped in disbelief. "Now, I have heard many of your comments about how the Johnson sisters gave generously of their time and money, and in their time of need the church could not help them. I would like to take a moment and address those concerns. Churches have limits on how much help they can provide to individuals and more importantly, the church is not here to take God's place; you must always look to Him for your answer. There are no limits to what God can do, and today I am happy to announce that on that same plane heading to London with Desiree Hunter are the Johnson sisters! Thanks to our incredible legal team, James and Betty Marshall, the Johnson sisters are also under contract with Millie Enterprises, and they will continue to lend their talent to the production of bags for Hunter Designs!" The church released a series of cheers and applause that went on for three full minutes. Pastor Lee did not want to stop them, but he had to move on with the morning service. It took another two minutes to finally settle them down. He normally would never address the church with gossip, but his congregation really needed to see how God came through for Katherine and Evelyn Johnson.

When the service ended, Pastor Lee returned to his office and met with Deacon Paul. The two men were about to order lunch when there was a knock on the door. Pastor Lee loosened his tie and picked up his mug of water, then reluctantly gave permission for the guests to enter. He was tired and was hoping to have a few minutes to eat before handling more duties. "Lee, may we speak with you privately?"

"Of course James and Betty, please come in. We were about to order lunch; would you two care to join us?"

"No thank you," replied Betty Marshall. Deacon Paul waited for Pastor Lee to ask him to leave; when that did not happen, he attempted to take some of the burden off of Pastor Lee.

"Can I be of service?" he asked, but James and Betty simply walked past him and sat down. Pastor Lee started out warm and friendly, but his spirit quickly told him they were here with trouble. He sat down slowly and began pushing his chair up to his desk as he looked curiously at the couple.

Betty Marshall spoke first. "As you know, Lee, my husband and I have been extremely generous to this church for quite some time. We handled the deed for the new community center, the tax issues, some of the congregation's personal matters, and recently my husband had to call in a few favors to get representation for Romeo. That kid has quite a rap sheet." Pastor Lee looked over at James Marshall, wondering why he was letting his wife do all the talking. "Now you know the latest contract we had to negotiate on Desiree's behalf was a huge challenge for us; with Desiree having no formal business training, no business plan or production crew, we had to work hard to cover up the fact that she is not even considered a small business owner. My husband and I spent countless days with the marketing and legal departments of Millie Enterprises."

Pastor Lee was growing inpatient. "I understand that wasn't exactly church business, but your husband and I already settled that payment issue."

"I know," replied Betty. "What we came to talk about is the new community center the church is about to open. My husband and I feel this would be a good time for the church to recognize our contributions in a greater way."

Pastor Lee was relieved. "Of course, Betty, in fact the committee was planning a special ceremony for all of our contributors; it was going to be a surprise."

James Marshall finally spoke up. "What my wife is trying to say is since the community center does not have a formal name yet, well, we wondered how the church would feel about naming the community center after us."

For the next few minutes, there was dead silence in the room. Pastor Lee regained his composure, and then asked in a questionable tone, "After you two?"

James leaned back in his chair, trying to show a confident demeanor, but his voice grew shaky as he spoke. "Lee, my wife and I have done a lot for this church; now we don't need the church's money, but we are the church's best investment, and it's time we get recognized."

Pastor Lee stood up and removed his glasses. "I'm sorry the two of you feel you are the church's best investment; even I can't make that claim. If you no longer feel called to serve this church, I will have to respect that, but I will not tolerate you threatening the security of this church, and believe me, James, I am being very kind with my choice of words."

Betty tapped her husband on the hand, signaling to him that she would now speak. "Lee, there's something you should know. There's a reporter by the name of Barrington who has been asking a lot of questions about you and your involvement with Hunter Designs; now we know he was acting on behalf of Sasha Montgomery, but the questions he's asking seem to be more about you, and they are rather personal. He is inquiring about your relationship with Desiree."

"So what?" replied Pastor Lee as his eyes remained fixed on James Marshall. "I spoke with Barrington several times myself. I told him everything he wanted to know about Hunter Designs. It was all business; it was completely legal, and not a dime of that money came from the church."

Betty hurried over to her purse and retrieved a newspaper clipping and set it down on the table. The headline read, "Millie Enterprises Makes a Surprise Visit to a New York Showcase." Under the headline was a picture of a fairly old white woman in a customized wheelchair.

"Do you see this, Lee?" Betty asked. "This sweet old woman is Mildred Montgomery, also known as Miss Millie; she is also the mother of Sasha Montgomery, who just happens to be the lead counsel for Millie Enterprises. These two ladies are on their way here to meet with us in two days."

"So what?" replied Pastor Lee.

Betty Marshall started to panic. "Lee, there is no need for Sasha Montgomery or her mother to come here. We met with their legal team days ago, and everything was all set, then suddenly we get a call saying Sasha Montgomery wants to meet with us. Now as much as I hate to admit this Lee, I am not looking forward to going a few rounds with Sasha Montgomery. I checked this woman out, and her reputation for winning difficult cases is well deserved. This woman has one of the sharpest legal minds in the profession. If her visit here has anything to do with Desiree possibly copying one of their designs, we could be in for some real trouble."

"Betty, if you have a point to make, this would be a good time to make it," said Pastor Lee.

Betty was now furious; unable to shake Pastor Lee's confidence, she simply stated, "My sources tell me we should be more than a little concerned by Sasha Montgomery's sudden interest in this deal."

"My wife is right, Lee; something more is bringing Sasha Montgomery here. Is it possible that Desiree could have copied one of their designs?"

Pastor Lee looked at the couple. "If either of you believed for one minute that Desiree copied one of their designs, you would have raced in here with that question, but you're too good of an attorney not to have already checked into that, James. Now, the two of you have wasted enough of my time."

"Please, Lee, just hear us out," pleaded James. "Miss Millie is a tough negotiator; we never expected her to agree to all the terms of Desiree's contract, but she did, and it's possible that Sasha Montgomery now wants to trim some of those benefits from the contract. If that's the reason for their visit, then the Johnson sisters could find themselves back here with no place to go."

"We will deal with Miss Millie and her daughter; you

and your wife will no longer have to worry about representing Desiree or this church!"

James Marshall stood up slowly, and in a very condescending manner he replied, "Let me clue you in on what we are up against, Lee." He took another article from his pocket and slammed it on the table. Pastor Lee kept his eyes on James while he slowly pushed the article back to him.

"There is nothing you can say that will change my mind James; now take your article and your wife and get out of my office."

Betty Marshall stood up and approached the two men. "Lee, you are making a big mistake; remember they are only giving Desiree's bags a trial run, and after that, the whole contract is up for renegotiation. If my husband does not represent Desiree, she could lose everything, and everyone will blame you."

"Well, then let them," replied Pastor Lee. At this point Deacon Paul decided the Marshalls had taken up enough of the Pastor's time; he got up and held the door open, expecting the Marshalls to take the hint, but instead of leaving, Betty Marshall stormed over toward him and slammed the door shut. She then snatched the article off the table and held it up to Pastor Lee's face. His wife's actions embarrassed James, and he quickly pulled the article back; then with a hint of compassion he pleaded, "Lee, do not be fooled by these two ladies. Betty did some research on Sasha Montgomery and found an interesting article on her. It seems some company was trying to strong arm an eighty-year-old widow into quitting. Apparently, the original owners of the company left the widow a nice retirement plan that the new owners did not want to honor. When the company instituted a new policy that required all of their employees to have the ability to speak a foreign language, the widow found herself out of a job. It made a lot of people angry, but the company's lawyers were good. When Miss Millie heard about it, she asked her daughter to step in. Sasha Montgomery took the case pro bono and won. The widow walked away with her retirement package and a whole lot more."

"That's great," replied Pastor Lee. "Now getting back to our business..."

"We have no more business," replied James Marshall. "My wife and I are officially withdrawing our legal support to the church, and we are no longer willing to represent Desiree. Good luck getting her deal finalized."

As the Marshalls made their way out of the office, James turned around and played his last and most powerful card. "Lee, you should know my wife made a last-minute change to Desiree's initial contract. There is now a clause that states we have the right to collect a portion of her income, whether she retains us as legal counsel or not. We went to see Desiree and her mother last night. Desiree didn't want to sign it, but her mother convinced her to do so. We expect to have the new contract in our office first thing tomorrow morning. Even if you find new representation for Desiree, it will cost her a small fortune to get out of her contract with us."

Deacon Paul could not believe what he had heard. "You and Betty would do that to Desiree?" he asked. "What kind of..." But before Deacon Paul could complete his sentence, Pastor Lee held up his hand, signaling Paul not to speak. James turned to Pastor Lee and asked, "Would you like to deliver this news to the congregation, or should we?" Pastor Lee managed to keep his composure when he spoke. "Now you listen to me, James, as your pastor, I am urging you to go home and find whatever door the enemy used to get you to this point before this dark influence destroys your marriage." Pastor Lee was about to suggest a counseling session for them, but they stormed out of the office and into the lounge, informing a few bystanders that Desiree's deal was off, thanks to the pastor.

Deacon Paul stood quietly in the corner of the office; his eyes were fixed on the article the Marshalls left behind. "Pastor, you should read this article."

Pastor Lee held up his hand and said, "Please, Paul, I've heard enough about Sasha Montgomery and her mother."

"You may want to hear this." Without waiting for permission, Deacon Paul read the last paragraph of the very long article. "Sasha Montgomery, lead counsel for Millie Enterprises, shocked the jury by putting her eighty-year-old client on the stand. Ms. Montgomery argued that the company wrongfully terminated her client, who did in fact speak a foreign language. While on the stand, Ms. Montgomery asked her client to tell the jury about her years of employment with the company. The elderly woman began speaking, and the jury was able to follow her story; minutes later the elderly woman began speaking in tongues. When Sasha Montgomery saw the confused look on the faces of the jury, she stood up and stated, 'Your Honor, I rest my case.'

Pastor Lee waited patiently for Paul to finish reading the article, then simply replied, "Let's get back to work, Paul; we have a lot of changes to make. The opening of the new community center will continue as planned, but the dedication ceremony will have to be put on hold."

Deacon Paul looked confused. "What about Desiree and the Johnson sisters? We can't just sit back and do nothing. It would be a shame if they were all forced back here." Pastor Lee walked back to his desk and sat down.

"This is not about Desiree or the Johnson sisters. The whole church worked hard to build this new community center. We have mothers who need our daycare center and homeless people who need food and medical attention."

"So we're just going to let the Marshalls ruin this opportunity for Desiree?" asked Deacon Paul.

Pastor Lee gave Deacon Paul a surprised look. "Do you honestly believe the Marshalls have the ability to stop God's plan?"

Paul became defensive. "I just meant it would cost the church a small fortune to obtain legal services for Desiree, and with so many of our legal matters still pending, we could stand to lose a lot."

"I know what's at stake Paul, but it doesn't matter. No one is stronger than the God we serve; you should know that by now. Let's call it a day and get some rest; we can finish this stuff up tomorrow."

Deacon Paul picked up the newspaper and studied the picture of Miss Millie. "Isn't it interesting how Miss Millie is always photographed, but we never see her daughter in any photos?" he asked.

"Well, it won't be hard to recognize her," replied Pastor Lee. "Our congregation is 99 percent black, so all we have to do is wait for the first white woman not in a wheelchair to come through those doors, and there we have her, Sasha Montgomery!" Both men laughed as they made their way out of the office and down the hall. "Darlene, we're leaving for the day. Do me a favor, please. Call Mike Rollins for me and tell him there has been a change of plans, and I want him to head up the boys' youth group. Oh, and there's one more call I need you to make. Call Henrietta and tell her to assemble the intercessors and ask her to wait for my call."

"Sure," replied Darlene. "Oh, wait, Pastor, this came

for you today." Darlene held up a beautiful gift basket. "Be sure to take the basket inside when you get home; I couldn't get to the store, and you are out of flavored tea, but there's some in the basket." Pastor Lee smiled. Darlene was so efficient and so thoughtful, and he could not imagine having to run the church without her.

"Who is the basket from?" he asked.

"It's from Ms. Sasha Montgomery."

Pastor Lee sighed as he took the gift basket and made his way out of the building.

Thirty minutes later, Pastor Lee pulled into his driveway; tired and hurt. He slowly walked to the door, unlocked it and threw his keys on the table. Suddenly his beautiful split level condo seemed so empty, something was missing and he knew what it was. Katherine Johnson was gone. Every night when he came home, she would call him and they would talk for hours. Most of the time their conversations were about church business, but they both knew it was more than that. Katherine was his friend, his helper and the only person who encouraged him during his trials. If only he had been able to let go of his pain and guilt of not being there to protect his wife Angela and their daughter Courtney, he would have made Katherine his wife; but he could not stand to fail again. Now he had to face this situation without Katherine's encouragement, without her smile or her laughter and most of all without her love.

Pastor Lee went upstairs to his study to retrieve his bible. He knew he needed to pray; he still had trouble accepting what the Marshall's had done and losing them was hard. They were more than the church's legal advisors, James Marshall was his friend; they played golf together, went fishing and he and Katherine often spent the holidays with them. But something changed and caused them to rebel, not just against him, but against God and their actions were threatening the security of the church and Desiree's future.

Pastor Lee went back downstairs and put the kettle on, then went and took a hot shower. A few minutes later, he emerged from his shower, dressed in his night clothes and rushed into the kitchen when he heard the teapot begin to whistle. As he reached into the cabinet, he found his wooden box of selected teas, empty. Now he remembered why Darlene told him to bring the gift basket inside. Darlene always placed his order of selected teas and had it shipped directly to his home, but this time she must have forgotten to place the order. Darlene was always so efficient and never missed a beat when it came to details, but things have been so crazy lately and with Katherine not there to take some of the work load off of Darlene, he realized this may become the new norm. He needed to have his tea, so he threw on a jogging suit and walked back out to his car and retrieved the gift basket. Pastor Lee was exhausted; the events of the day left him weary and feeling empty. Looking over the contents of the gift basket, he was surprised to see French crumpets, bread, cheese, fresh fruit, nuts, and flavored tea in the basket; there was also a mini serving tray, a teapot and two cups with saucers. Sasha Montgomery spared no expense with this basket, it was such a welcomed gift, that he almost forgot how much trouble her visit was causing. He opened the basket and pulled out a box of tea. At this point it didn't matter what flavor it was; he just needed something hot. As he sat down and placed his cup of tea on the table, he could no longer ignore the pain caused by the Marshalls, and he began to cry out. "Lord, what is happening? In all my years of pastoring, this church, I have never encountered such betrayal. I know the enemy has slipped into our church and the Marshalls are being used to take us down. This hurts, Lord, and I have no idea how to get the church out of this mess." Pastor Lee then got down on his knees and prayed. "Lord, my shoulders are heavy, and my strength is weak. I know you did not allow your servants to come this far without a plan to take them all the way. Give me strength, Lord, as I wait for your deliverance, and help me keep my congregation faithful as they witness this attack on your servants." While Pastor Lee was still on the floor praying, he reached up to retrieve his Bible and accidentally knocked it to the floor. The Bible opened, and his eyes fell onto a scripture he had recently highlighted, *Be still and know that I am God. Psalm 46:10.* Pastor Lee smiled, and with an incredible sense of relief, he lifted himself up and sat down at his kitchen table. At that very moment, he knew God was speaking to him and he knew everything was going to be okay.

The tea was still hot, so he took a sip and immediately spit it out. Of all the flavors he could have picked, he could not believe he ended up with raspberry-flavored tea. The only thing worse than drinking this tea was the thought of staying up any longer to make another cup, so he poured the tea down the sink and went upstairs to bed.

CHAPTER SEVENTEEN

The morning came quickly, and Pastor Lee woke early. There was so much work to be done today; in addition to finding new counsel for the church, he also needed to replace many of the vacant positions he now had. Pastor Lee sat down and read his Bible. After an hour he decided to check the messages on his answering machine; each time the caller made reference to the rumors about Desiree coming back home, he just deleted the message. The last message was a call he was happy to return, and he quickly dialed Carl's number.

Carl answered immediately. "Sorry to hear about the Marshalls. Is there anything I can do?"

Pastor Lee had such a strong level of respect for Carl. It was no secret he wanted nothing more than to have Carl sit on the church's board, but Carl was not open to the idea. "No, Carl, this battle is too big for us; we have to put this one in God's hands."

"I understand, replied Carl. "But I did want to talk to you about Desiree's revised contract."

Pastor Lee sighed. "The Marshalls already got her to sign it, and there's nothing we can do, Carl."

"Well, that's what I'm calling about; Desiree brought the revised contract to me before she left. Her mother told her to sign it, but she didn't think it was fair, so she asked me to look it over. I read it, and told her not to sign it."

"Are you sure, Carl?"

"Yes, I have the unsigned contract with me now."

"Carl, I don't know what to say, except God has given us our first win of the day!"

"Well, we're not out of the woods yet," replied Carl. "The Marshalls are likely to still challenge us. I just want you to know that you're not in this alone, Pastor; the whole church is behind you."

"Thank you, Carl, I appreciate that."

Pastor Lee hung up and was feeling better already. Glancing over at the clock, he noticed it was already seven o'clock, and he needed to get going; he dressed quickly, then packed up his collection of books to donate to the center and headed out the door.

As he pulled into the staff parking lot, Pastor Lee looked around; it was still early, and he did not expect anyone to be here, but there were already several cars in the parking lot. This type of support warmed his heart; but that warmness quickly faded as he entered the building, and found most of the staff feeding each other details about what the Marshalls had done; not one of them was actually engaged in their duties. What disturbed him the most was seeing Deacon Paul in the midst of them. Pastor Lee looked around for Darlene, and found her locked in his office. It was no surprise to him that Darlene would have removed herself from the gossip. "Good morning, Pastor Lee, your coffee is brewing, and your mail is on the table. Oh, and I made something for you and Deacon Paul to nibble on."

Darlene stood up and smiled at him. "Well, how do you like the way I decorated your office?"

Pastor Lee looked around; there were too many plants for his liking, and the pictures Darlene hung were too formal for his taste. Katherine would have hung better ones, he thought to himself. "My office looks great, Darlene, thank you."

"I'm glad you like it; I'll get out of your way now. Oh, and don't forget your first appointment is with Ms. Montgomery at ten o'clock this morning. I pushed all of your other meetings back to this afternoon."

"Ten o'clock today Darlene? My appointment with Ms. Montgomery is scheduled for tomorrow at 11:30 a.m., not today."

Darlene gave him a puzzling look. "Sasha Montgomery called this morning and said the appointment couldn't wait until tomorrow; she said she was certain you would make time for her today. I am sorry. I just assumed she spoke with you already."

"How would I have spoken to her, Darlene?"

"I'm sorry, Pastor, but there were so many people calling here this morning, I guess I got mixed up."

Pastor Lee sighed. "I guess its best we get this meeting out of the way, and I'm sorry, Darlene. I didn't mean to take anything out on you."

"I'll close the door so you're not disturbed," she said.

Pastor Lee sat down behind his desk. It felt good sitting in his own office instead of the tiny room he had in the church. Just as he picked up his cup of coffee and began to go through his mail, Deacon Paul came in. "Good morning, Paul, come in, and let's get started. Darlene just made a fresh pot of coffee; would you like a cup?"

"Sure, thank you." Paul sat down and nervously cleared his throat. "Pastor, before we get started, I feel I should inform you on what's going on with our congregation. Everyone is convinced that Desiree is on her way back home, and they want to know what is being done for her. I made a few phone calls last night, and we have a few possibilities for legal representation for the church, but we came up empty on a firm willing to represent Desiree. Apparently the fact that she has a contract with an international company presents a big challenge. Most firms simply don't see a big enough payoff to get involved." Pastor Lee began eating his breakfast. "What are we going to do?" asked Deacon Paul.

"I wish I knew," responded Pastor Lee.

"Well, are you at least going to address this before the congregation on Sunday?"

"Absolutely not. Sunday's service will go according to plan; this turn of events will not move us. Are you sure you don't want some breakfast? It's amazing how Darlene can take something as simple as oatmeal and turn it into a gourmet meal."

Pastor Lee's calmness continued to baffle Deacon Paul. "No, thank you. I guess I'll start moving these boxes into the library while you finish your breakfast."

At that moment Darlene's voice came through the intercom. "Excuse me, Pastor Lee, but you have a visitor."

The two men looked at each other. "I thought Darlene kept your schedule clear this morning," said Paul.

"I thought so too," replied Pastor Lee, and then he pressed the button on the intercom and responded, "Thank you, Darlene. I'll be out in a few minutes." He turned off the intercom and said, "Well, so much for getting any work done this morning."

"Would you like me to handle it?" Paul asked.

"No, I'll go out, but it would help to know who is out there. Darlene never said who was waiting to see me."

"Why don't you finish your breakfast? I'll go greet them and buy you some time."

"Thanks, Paul, I would appreciate that."

Before Paul could get to the door, Darlene came

rushing in and closed the door behind her. "Pastor! You are not going to believe this, but Miss Millie herself is in the lobby!"

"Please tell me you're joking," he replied. "You said Sasha Montgomery was arriving at ten o'clock this morning, you said nothing about Miss Millie."

"Well, I can ask her to come back at ten o'clock," replied Darlene. "Maybe she got the time mixed up too."

"I doubt it," replied Pastor Lee. "I don't know why these two women believe they can decide how and when to use my time. Please let Miss Millie know I will be out in a few minutes." Pastor Lee stood up and put his jacket on. As he walked down the hall, he tried to recall the many things he heard about this ruthless icon and what a shrewd business woman she was. What nerve she had to show up early and expect him to see her. As he approached the lounge, he saw an elderly white woman in a wheelchair. She had a very graceful appearance, unlike the hardened business woman he was expecting to see. Standing next to her was an attractive young woman who appeared to be her assistant. The young woman was busy securing a shawl around Miss Millie's shoulders. With her back toward Pastor Lee, the young woman did not see him until he was standing directly behind her and said hello. Startled, she turned around and immediately took several steps back; she gave Pastor Lee an intense stare, then struggled to bring forth a warm but nervous smile before quickly excusing herself. Pastor Lee extended his hand to Miss Millie, who sat quietly but also gave him the same intense stare. "Is Sasha Montgomery on her way?" he asked. "I thought I was meeting with her this morning."

Miss Millie's voice was strained. "Yes, Pastor Lee, you will have a meeting with my daughter very soon. Is there someplace we can talk in private? It's very important."

"Certainly," he replied. "We can go into my office. Do you need some help?"

"No, I'm fine, thank you."

As they made their way back to his office, Pastor Lee started to relax. His spirit was at peace with this woman, and he realized she was not elderly at all. Her face told the story of a woman who was holding onto pain, and her pain was reflected in both her eyes and in her drained facial expression. He held the door to his office open, and Miss Millie went in.

"Can I offer you a cold drink or some coffee?"

Miss Millie put her hand up but never spoke in response to his offer. He picked up a glass and began filling it with water, then sat down at the table. "It's very nice to meet you, Miss Millie; let me apologize for not getting back to you. I know your office called several times about Miss Hunter's bags but..."

Miss Millie rudely cut in. "I think I'll have some water, please." Pastor Lee stared at her for a moment, then went into the café and returned with a cold bottle of water and a glass and placed it on the table. "Thank you," she said. Pastor Lee then took notice of Miss Millie's demeanor; she was clearly anxious and seemed uncomfortable in his presence, which was not quite the reaction he expected from such a ruthless tycoon.

He tried to lighten the mood and jokingly said to her, "My secretary would be surprised to know I was able to find my way around the café."

Miss Millie did not smile or acknowledge his humor; instead, she looked around disapprovingly. "No place for people in wheelchairs?"

Her comment puzzled him; it appeared she wanted to make small talk and seemed to have something other than Desiree's business deal on her mind. "Actually, we do have a ramp outside, and since the community center is all one level, there really is no need for additional ramps. Now, Miss Millie, I believe I know why you're here."

"I doubt it," she replied, taking a sip of water. "I'd rather have tea. Do you have any tea?"

"Sure," he replied, wondering why she had not asked for tea in the first place. This time he pushed the button on the intercom and asked Darlene to bring in a cup of tea. After several minutes, Darlene entered the office with a hot cup of tea and a tea biscuit and sat them down in front of Miss Millie.

"Will there be anything else?" she asked.

"No, Darlene. I think Miss Millie is fine now, thank you." Pastor Lee cleared his throat. "Miss Millie, I have to tell you that our church unfortunately has lost its legal representation, and I'm afraid we just haven't found anyone to represent Desiree. I asked my secretary to call your office..."

Miss Millie cut in again. "I know all about your legal troubles, and I think the position your legal team has taken with your church is a very sad one. I want you to know we are fully prepared to sign Ms. Hunter and take her on as one of our designers."

Millie took an envelope from the side of her wheelchair and gently pushed it toward him. "As you know, her initial contract would have allowed us to test her bags in a few of our stores before making a full commitment. What you have there is a new contract, and it is a very clear and simple one. If Ms. Hunter accepts our offer, she will create the bags exclusively for us; she can retain the use of her own name on her designs. Take a look at the bottom line; you will see our offer is quite generous."

Pastor Lee looked down at the monetary figure being offered. He was stunned but remained composed. "This is a very generous offer. I wasn't aware Desiree's bags could command that type of money."

"They can't," replied Miss Millie. "Ms. Hunter's bags are beautiful, and we can sell them, but my company is not in the market for evening bags at this time. In fact, it was my daughter Sasha who wanted to test Desiree's line of teacup bags. You can imagine my surprise when we learned this designer produced these bags in this church's basement. Moving her to London was the only way we could get the quantities we need for our stores. I still can't believe she was able to produce such a nice product with only the help of the Johnson sisters."

Pastor Lee smiled. "I see you have done your homework on us."

"Not me," replied Miss Millie. "It was a young journalist my daughter met in New York. If it weren't for him, we may never have found you."

"You mean you would never have found Desiree?"

Miss Millie looked at him. "No, I mean you. Excuse me, Pastor. I have to make myself a note." Miss Millie took out a pad and pen and began writing. Pastor Lee sensed this woman was stalling. James Marshall was right; something more brought this woman here, and now he wanted to know what she was really after. "Do you know Barrington?" Miss Millie asked.

"No, I can't say I know Barrington personally, but I have spoken to him several times. He is quite the investigative reporter," said Pastor Lee with a laugh.

"Yes, I heard that as well," replied Millie. "That's why I want to meet the young man and see if I can convince him to work for us."

Pastor Lee did not want to offend her, but he needed to wrap this meeting up. There was no need for him to meet with Sasha Montgomery; it was clear that the offer from Miss Millie was God's answer to this part of his problem. Now he needed to move on with his day. Taking a deep breath, he asked in a gentle tone, "Miss Millie did you come all this way to confirm this offer in person?"

"No, of course not!" she snapped. "My time is much more valuable than that. I'm here because of my daughter Sasha, who by the way you just met."

Now it was Pastor Lee who rudely cut in. "Your daughter?" he asked in a curious tone. "You mean the young lady who was with you in the lobby is your daughter?"

Miss Millie smiled. "Its okay, Pastor. I have spent a lifetime with people assuming I could not be Sasha's mother because Sasha is black. I adopted her when she was eight years old, but adoption did not make Sasha my daughter; love did."

Pastor Lee was not sure why Miss Millie was explaining all of this to him, but it was the sort of thing people did all the time. "That's a beautiful sentiment, Miss Millie, and one that is all too often forgotten." Pastor Lee paused before continuing. "Miss Millie, I don't understand; if that was Sasha Montgomery, then why didn't she join us for the meeting? The Marshalls have dealt us a blow, and unfortunately, we are not out of the woods with Desiree's contract. I hope I'm not taking on too much by assuming Sasha Montgomery would help us?"

"Don't worry about your former legal team," ordered Miss Millie. "If they challenge us, my daughter will mop the floor with them!" Miss Millie began dusting crumbs off of her lap as she continued to enjoy the tea biscuit.

"Yes, I've heard so much about the infamous Sasha Montgomery; you must be very proud of her."

At that very moment, Millie hung her head and sobbed. Pastor Lee waited patiently for a few minutes;

he wanted to see if she would tell him what was upsetting her or if he was going to have to pull the information out of her. He knew something else caused this woman to travel here, and he was about to find out what it was. "Miss Millie, I want you to take a deep breath and tell me what's troubling you."

Millie took a pack of tissues from her purse, and with a long, deep breath she began. "One afternoon my husband and I were driving into town when the car ahead of us made a sudden turn. Out of nowhere came a dusty blue 1979 Chevy. It hit the car ahead of us at full speed." Miss Millie was now rocking forward and backwards as she struggled with the next set of details. "The impact immediately killed the driver, at least that's what the police said." Pastor Lee struggled to hear her; for years he avoided any talk of car accidents until he came into the ministry, where he was forced to confront it. There were not too many 1979 Chevys left, and yet here this woman from another country was bringing his nightmare back to him. His body tensed up as he wondered who this woman was and why she was here. "There was a little girl in the car; she was screaming and calling for her mother. Someone pulled the little girl from the car; she was hysterical. My husband ran to the car to help, but before he could check on the driver, the car that hit them came back." Miss Millie was now crying, with only the boundaries of the wheelchair preventing her from falling out of her chair. "The drunk driver got out of the car and began stumbling toward my husband. When the man saw what he had done, he stumbled back to his car; he was so drunk he was tripping over himself. He got into his car, and as drunk as he was, he probably thought he was moving forward, but instead he put the car in reverse and sped backward. There was a crowd of people yelling for my husband to move out of the way, but the little girl was only a few feet from the drunk driver. My husband threw his body over the little girl and saved her life. They were both taken to the emergency room, Arthur recovered and did not suffer any long term injuries but the little girl remained traumatized." Miss Millie's face was now completely red, and her supply of tissues had run out. Pastor Lee's stomach felt like he had been hit with a ton of bricks. He couldn't speak, his hands were sweaty, his eyes burned, and his head was spinning. He picked up the glass of water he had given to Miss Millie, but he couldn't bring himself to drink it. "I was told I went into a state of shock and woke up in a hospital a couple of days later. We were all alone, you know. Arthur was a doctor and he loved kids, but we couldn't have any, so the children at the hospital were his little ones. For the next few weeks, I wondered about the little girl. I started asking around, but no one wanted to give information about a little black girl to some old white woman. Eventually, I located the detective who handled the case, and he told me an aunt had come to take the little girl, so I figured she was okay, but God kept speaking to me. I can't explain it, but you're a pastor, so you must know what I'm saying. For days I had no peace. I couldn't sleep or eat; somehow I knew this little girl was still in trouble and that I was supposed to find her."

Pastor Lee sat with his face in his hands; his eyes were filled with tears. Suddenly, he recalled the intense stare of Sasha Montgomery; she had his wife's eyes. Could this be the daughter he believed for? Then he remembered the gift basket; it all made sense now. It was filled with raspberry tea; that was his daughter's favorite tea. When she was a little girl, she would invite him to her tea parties, where she made him sit down at her tiny table and drink raspberry tea with her make-believe friends. With the tears streaming down his face, he remembered his daughter scolding him for showing up to her tea parties empty handed, so he started sending her small gift baskets whenever he received an invitation to one of her tea parties. The gift basket filled with raspberry tea was no coincidence; his daughter sent that basket to let him know who she was.

Pastor Lee struggled to stand, and as soon as he took his first step, he fell to the floor sobbing uncontrollably. Millie got up out of her wheelchair and went to comfort him. Lying in the arms of the woman who had his daughter all these years, he was too afraid to ask her who Sasha Montgomery really was. He wanted to hear her say it, but he needed to guard his heart. He called out to God.

"Please, Lord, tell me this is her. Please let it be true, God. Are you really giving me my daughter back?" Pastor Lee could hear the echo of a sermon he preached only weeks ago, about a man who lost everything. As he lay crying on the floor, he kept asking, "Is this you, God; is this really you?"

Pastor Lee knew God was speaking to him, the words were strong on his heart, but he was too emotional to hear God. All this time he was helping Desiree, he only did it, out of obedience to God. He never saw this blessing coming. Suddenly he heard the words from his previous sermon. The words hit his heart with an incredible amount of joy. *Hear this, O Job; stop and consider the wondrous works of God. Job 37:14.* But Pastor Lee wanted to hear more; he wanted reassurance this was really God answering his prayers. He knew in his heart, who Sasha Montgomery really was, but he wanted to keep hearing it over and over; he continued to cry hysterically while on the floor, then he asked. "Who was she, Millie? Who was that young woman with you?"

Millie smiled and looked down at him; she held his head in her arms and wiped the tears from his eyes, then she whispered in his ear, "That young lady is your daughter, Courtney Shields."

ABOUT THE AUTHOR

Emerald Moore was born and raised in Bronx, New York; she graduated from Evander Childs High School and went on to earn a degree in communications from Elizabeth Seton College in Yonkers, New York.

Emerald began her career in print media in 1997 when she launched, *My Favorite Book,* a company that created books for school fundraisers. The success of that company inspired her to reach for something more personal. Emerald's love for God inspired her to write for His glory.

Shoes on the Bridge (Meet the Family) is the first in this series. While the characters and situations in this book are fictional; the way God moves in the lives of people is real.

Emerald now lives in New Jersey and is currently working on the next series of Shoes on the Bridge.

Shoes on the Bridge, is available on Amazon.com.

Direct all inquiries to:Shoesonthebridge@gmail.com